THE FRENCH ISLES

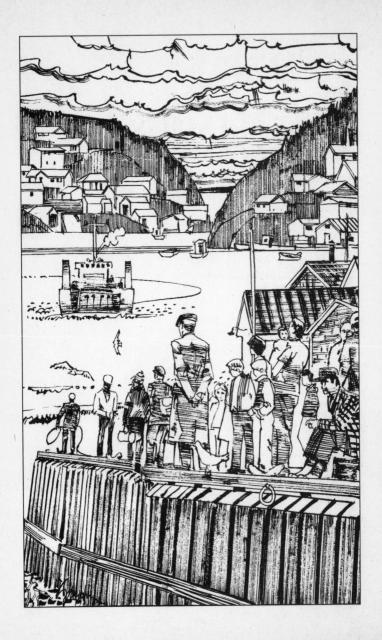

CLAIRE MOWAT

THE FRENCH ISLES

Illustrations by

Huntley Brown

SEAL BOOKS
McClelland-Bantam, Inc.
Toronto

For Jack and Elizabeth McClelland

This edition contains the complete text
of the original hardcover edition.
NOT ONE WORD HAS BEEN OMITTED.

THE FRENCH ISLES
A Seal Book/Published by arrangement with Key Porter Books
PUBLISHING HISTORY
Key Porter edition published 1994
Seal edition / December 1995
CIP: C94-931208-8

For information address: Key Porter Books Limited, 70 The
Esplanade, Toronto, Ontario M5E 1R2, Canada

ISBN 0-770-42719-7

PRINTED IN U.S.A.
FFG   0 9 8 7 6 5 4 3 2 1

CHAPTER ONE

"WHERE ON EARTH IS SIERRA LEONE?" ASKED Andrea.

She had been in her bedroom sitting at her desk trying to finish her homework, although she had actually been thinking about her toe-nails. She didn't like the cinnamon-coloured nail polish she had painted them last week and was wondering if a deep pink shade might look better. That was when her mother had interrupted her with this bombshell.

"It's nowhere I've ever been, my dear, that's for sure. It's in Africa. The west coast of Africa—a place I never thought I'd live to see," replied her mom dreamily.

"But why would you want to go there for six months?" asked Andrea, bewildered.

"Sweetie, we have to stay that long in order to get the job done. Try and understand that there's a need for teachers, for people with certain skills who can make a difference in that place. It's an opportunity for us to see another part of the world. You see, Brad has always wanted to do this kind of thing, to go to —"

"Oh, I might have known it would be Brad's idea! He's just full of great ideas, isn't he?" Andrea shouted angrily and stomped out of the room, slamming the door behind her.

Brad was her stepfather. He and her mom were both teachers. They had been married for only a few months and already he wanted to change things. When he moved

1

in, he brought his CD player and tons of opera music, along with all his books and bookshelves and two really ugly paintings. Now the living-room was so crowded there was hardly room to sit down. He kept saying he wanted the three of them to move out of their apartment in the Toronto suburb of Willowdale and buy a house in the country somewhere. He used to have a really neat sports car and then all of a sudden he sold it and bought a stupid van. And now the latest—he wanted to go to Africa and teach school in some weird place. Andrea wished her mother had never married him. She wished she had never even heard of Bradley Osborne.

"Now, is that a nice way to behave?" her mother scolded, following Andrea through the living-room to the little balcony that was Andrea's favourite place to go when she was mad.

"I guess not," Andrea finally replied after a gloomy silence.

"You know how Brad is," her mom said in a soothing voice. "He wants to see the world and he believes we have to help people who haven't been as lucky as we are. And he's right. Think how fortunate we are. We have everything we need, and even money left over for eating out on Friday nights."

Andrea had to admit that once in a while Brad was okay, especially the times they ate out at Alberto's restaurant, where you could get the best pizza in Canada, and the best spumoni ice-cream in the world, and even a second helping if you wanted one.

"Yeah, I know, Mom. I know all that," Andrea

muttered. "It's just that . . . Africa? What about me? Am I supposed to come, or what?"

"That's what we have to talk about. We'd love it if you came with us. You'd be more than welcome. But there are a few . . . well, a few challenges. This particular place where we're going has no secondary school. We'll be teaching people who have never had a chance to get an education. There's been political unrest and there are a lot of refugees. There's a housing shortage so we could be living in a tent for a while. But if you do come with us, you could complete your school year by correspondence from Canada. And, of course, you'd have Brad and me there to help you, in the evenings."

"By candlelight, I suppose," said Andrea sarcastically.

"Probably lamplight or something like that."

"Ugh."

"Don't you be saucy, young lady! When I was your age, back in Newfoundland, we had lots of winter storms that knocked out the electricity. Plenty of times we did *our* homework by lamplight and we got along just fine," said her mother firmly.

"Well, it didn't happen last Christmas when I was there," Andrea countered.

"They've got better technology nowadays," her mother explained. "And that brings me to the other possibility. You did enjoy being there in Anderson's Arm last Christmas when Brad and I were away on our honeymoon, didn't you? You told me you did."

"Yup," nodded Andrea. At first, she had been reluctant to go to the Newfoundland outport her parents had come from but, as things turned out, it had really been a lot of fun.

"You know, you could spend those months in Anderson's Arm. I've been talking to your Aunt Pearl and Uncle Cyril on the phone. They said they'd love to have you stay with them. Your cousins think you're the greatest. I'm just asking you to think it over for a few days," concluded her mother in a tone of voice that Andrea knew meant serious business. Then she gave Andrea a hug.

"Okay, I will, Mom," Andrea promised, a little reluctantly.

"That's my girl. I know this is tough. Don't forget, you're the most important person in the world for me. It's just that there are so many people out there. Brad and I want to help wherever we can."

What kind of place was Sierra Leone? Andrea wondered. Her mother had brought home a couple of library books about west Africa. Frankly, thought Andrea, the pictures didn't make the place seem very appealing. The houses looked beige and dusty. Some of the people didn't wear shoes. Her mom said they ate a lot of rice and peanuts and sweet potatoes. Andrea didn't like sweet potatoes at all.

A couple of days later, she got a letter from her aunt Pearl Baxter. It was full of news about Uncle Cyril, who was going to buy a boat, and about her cousins, and lots of other people she had met in Anderson's Arm the previous Christmas. There were even some photographs Aunt Pearl had taken with the camera Uncle Cyril had given her then. Andrea felt sort of homesick for all of them. They had been so nice to her.

In the end, it wasn't so difficult to make up her mind. When it came to a choice between Sierra Leone, Africa, or Anderson's Arm, Newfoundland, Anderson's Arm was the hands-down winner. She would certainly miss her mother but all the other Baxters were family, too. Six whole months! She looked at her clothes closet and began thinking about what she should take with her.

"Andrea's mother was always the brazen one, wasn't she, Cyril?" remarked Pearl. Andrea was sitting between Aunt Pearl and Uncle Cyril in the front seat of her uncle's new truck. He called it his "new" truck but it must have been at least five years old. He had bought it a month earlier from a car dealer in Gander, the town where they had just collected Andrea at the airport.

"Yes, girl. Your mother was some smart and that's the truth. Soon as she married Albert, seemed like the pair of them couldn't wait to git going down the road," added Cyril as he steered his rattling truck along the Trans-Canada Highway.

Albert Baxter, Andrea's real father, had been dead a long time now—over seven years—but Andrea remembered him with love. Cyril, his brother, was her favourite uncle. He was a man who loved to make people laugh,

and he looked and acted quite a bit like her dad.

"But neither of *us* wanted to leave," explained Aunt Pearl. "We could never be content if we lived away, Cyril and me. The Arm is where we belong."

"People are like trees," declared Uncle Cyril thoughtfully. "Some can be dug up, roots and all, and moved to another place and they flourish finest kind. But others now, you dig them up and try to plant them somewhere else, and they just wilt and die."

"I'd say Andrea takes after her mother," smiled Aunt Pearl. "Content wherever she be—Toronto or Anderson's Arm."

"I guess so," agreed Andrea. But when she thought about it for a while, she wasn't too sure. What would it *really* be like spending such a long time with her relatives in a small outport?

Cyril Baxter turned off the highway along the coast road. Gradually a blanket of grey fog crept towards them. Uncle Cyril turned on the lights and reduced his speed. It became cooler. Andrea reached for her black leather jacket and wriggled into it. It was her very favourite jacket, a Christmas present from her mom last year.

She started thinking about her mother, soon to be far away in some place that was terribly hot. It dawned on her that her mother must be brave. At first, Andrea had just been angry—angry at Brad because it had been his idea to go to Africa, angry that her mom didn't simply tell him to forget it and refuse to go. But the more she thought about them, about the difficulties of teaching school in such a place, the more she began to realize that it wouldn't be easy for them either. Staying with her aunt and uncle and cousins was no big deal in comparison. It was easier than trying to live in a tent in Africa.

"I hope you likes t'eat scallops," remarked Uncle Cyril, interrupting her reverie.

"They're okay. I tried them a couple of times. Back home, Mom and Brad and I used to eat out every Friday night. Mom was always tired after teaching all week so we'd go to different restaurants, sometimes Italian, sometimes Chinese, sometimes seafood. That's where I tried scallops. The restaurant was called The Twin Mermaids. It had a sign out in the front with two mermaids swimming, sort of like synchronized swimming. It was neat," Andrea reminisced.

"Hah! I don't say you'll be eating in them places now, not in Anderson's Arm," laughed Cyril, "but soon as fishin' season begins, you'll get all the scallops you can eat, free of charge."

"We're some lucky," explained Aunt Pearl, "that Cyril got a licence to fish for scallops. These times there's no codfish to speak of but it seems there are scallops to be found out in the bay."

"Got me own boat now, maid," added Cyril proudly.

Maid. Would they ever stop calling her a maid? Andrea wondered. She knew what they meant, though. Maid was their word for a young girl. It didn't mean she was a maid who cleaned houses or hotels the way it did in Toronto. Of course, she was no stranger to housework. She had always helped her mother because, ever since she could remember, her mom had been teaching school and didn't have time to do everything herself. Andrea had learned early in life that she had to help tidy up the mess in the kitchen, make her bed, and get the laundry into the washer and then the dryer, and remember not to mix the white clothes with the coloured ones.

The road got bumpier the closer they got to Anderson's Arm. And the fog got thicker. Andrea was still daydreaming about her mother. She started remembering Friday nights, and all the fun they had deciding where they wanted to go to eat. For a few seconds she even thought about Brad in a kindly way. Then she was afraid she was going to cry. She didn't say a word for a long time. Her mood had grown as grey as the fog.

"Spring of the year we always gets the mauzy days," sighed Aunt Pearl, peering through her glasses at the wet, hazy world that lay ahead of them.

Spring? Was this supposed to be spring? Andrea wondered. It was the middle of June. It had been summer when she left Toronto that morning on her flight for Newfoundland. And what did "mauzy" mean, anyway? It had to mean wet or foggy or misty. They had so many strange words to describe things here, even the weather.

As Uncle Cyril's truck chugged resolutely up the hill and turned a corner, Andrea was able to make out the dim profile of the Baxters' trim wooden house through the mist. The truck ground to a halt in front of it. Uncle Cyril turned off the engine and they climbed out just as a fog-horn wailed mournfully in the distance. For one dark moment, Andrea wasn't sure if she had made the right decision after all.

CHAPTER TWO

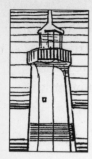

"THERE'S NOT MUCH TO DO AROUND HERE, IS there?" lamented Andrea to her cousin Jeff.

"Plenty to do," answered Jeff matter-of-factly. "We got to get this deck painted before tomorrow. Forecast calls for rain." Jeff was serious about the job. He had just turned thirteen and was more than a year younger than Andrea. He had straight dark hair and freckles on his nose. Andrea had light brown hair which was naturally wavy and got curlier when it was wet. She was now slightly taller than he was. In the past six months, she had grown faster than he had.

Andrea, Jeff, and her other cousin Matthew, who was only ten, had almost finished painting the new porch that Uncle Cyril had recently built on the back of the house. The boys called it a deck, even though Andrea kept insisting it was a porch.

When it was time to stop for supper, they took their paint brushes down to the "store," which was really a shed, where Cyril kept his fishing gear. They swished the paint remaining in each brush on the old door of the shed. Then they left the brushes to soak in a can half full of turpentine. People had been cleaning their paint brushes on the old door for years, leaving a rainbow of colours. Now it looked like one of the abstract paintings that Brad had hung in their living-room. Andrea was going to mention this similarity to the boys but decided not to in case they laughed at her.

"When we're finished painting—like tonight, after supper—what're we going to do then?" she asked, returning to her earlier complaint.

"I'm going over to Levi's house tonight. I promised to help him mend lobster traps," said Jeff.

"I think I'll watch TV," added Matthew. " 'Northwood High' is on."

"Oh. I guess I'll wash my hair then," said Andrea without enthusiasm.

Back at the house, Aunt Pearl had put their supper on the table. There was cold meat, potato salad, and pickles, with ginger cake for dessert, and lots of tea. Andrea hadn't been too fond of tea until she visited Anderson's Arm last Christmas but now she decided she liked it.

"I wish there was something to do or some place to go," she remarked to no one in particular.

"Could be I got just the ticket for you, maid," declared her uncle.

"Oh, what's that?" Andrea asked.

"I'm looking for a crew to fetch my new boat."

"You mean to go fishing?" asked Andrea, horrified. She didn't care for fishing at all.

"Can I go, Dad? Can I?" pleaded Jeff.

"Me too? Me too?" Matthew begged.

"No, not to go fishing. Not yet. First, I got to collect me new boat from the feller what sold it to me. Jeff, you're big enough now so you can come along to spell me off at the wheel. Matt, you got to bide home and keep things shipshape here. There's room for one more and we need somebody who can cook," announced Cyril.

Andrea looked over at Aunt Pearl. "Aren't you going to go?"

"Don't say as I will. I never was one for going about in boats," replied Pearl. "Looks to me like Cyril has you in mind for the job."

"You said you wanted to go somewhere, didn't you?" Jeff reminded her. "And you knows how to cook, don't you?"

"Of course I can cook—well, sort of. But I'm not altogether crazy about boats myself," she added uncertainly. "How far away is this place anyway?"

"A nice ways," said Cyril, stroking his chin. "Wilfred's Harbour is on the southwest coast. No road down there."

"No road? How do you get there?" asked Andrea, surprised.

"On the water," laughed Cyril. "What else would a boat float on?"

"I know that." Andrea felt a bit silly. "I know you'll be sailing your boat back on the ocean. What I meant was how do we get to Wilfred's Harbour in the first place? Is there an airport?"

"Airport?" snorted Cyril. "Only way to get to Wilfred's Harbour is aboard the coast boat. We drive down to Bay d'Espoir and then we get aboard the steamer, as we used to call her. That's how it was around here when I was a youngster. No road to Anderson's Arm them times."

"This, um, coast boat. Is it big?" enquired Andrea.

"Big enough. Bunks to sleep in. Hot meals, too. But not near so big as those old steamers was. You mind, Pearl? There was the *Bonavista* and the *Burgeo* and the *Baccalieu*," Cyril reminisced, reciting the names of ships that had sailed into Anderson's Arm a long time ago.

"I was wondering," Andrea began thoughtfully, "those boats—are they like the Love Boat? You know, on television? With a captain in a white uniform and dancing in the evening and all that stuff?"

"Dancing?" laughed Aunt Pearl. "I never heard tell of anyone dancing on the coast boat unless it was dancing with joy to get where they was going. Wonderful stormy in the winter, I can tell you."

"You can be sure they has a captain," Cyril laughed. "Finest kind of skippers, too. They knows the ocean better than any fish."

"Wish I could go," grumbled Matthew.

"Bide your time, my son. When you're bigger, we'll fish together. That's a promise," Cyril consoled him. "Don't take on now. We won't be gone more'n a few days. What about it, maid?" he asked Andrea.

"Well, if you're not too fussy, I suppose I could be the cook," Andrea agreed haltingly.

"Can you make a sandwich? Open a can of soup? Boil the kettle for a mug-up?" asked her uncle, outlining the job requirements.

"Oh, sure, I can do that. Whenever Mom had to work late I used to get supper ready."

"There you go then!" exclaimed her aunt. "'Twould be something to write and tell your mother about."

"True," nodded Andrea. "There's not much else happening here to write about."

Mr. Noseworthy, who lived in the next house along the road, owned a van in which he collected the mail and hauled things from one place to another, and sometimes he used it as a taxi. He agreed to drive Cyril, Jeff, and Andrea to a town called St. Alban's, which was located on the shore of a huge bay in the south of Newfoundland. It was a long drive through a landscape of small trees, enormous rocks, and large ponds. Once they saw a big brown moose wandering near the road. They stopped the van for a minute to look while the moose walked lazily away and disappeared into the forest. Andrea thought this was very exciting. She had seen one before at the Metro Toronto Zoo but it was altogether different to see such a big animal in a place where it was free to roam wherever it wanted to go.

It took most of the day to reach St. Alban's and then they had to wait several hours on the wide government wharf for the coast boat to arrive. It sailed in just before dusk, a modern-looking, diesel-powered vessel, about the length of a Toronto Island ferry but streamlined like the cruise ship on television. Cyril watched it intently as it eased up to the wharf.

"That skipper knows what he's about," he said with admiration, "but all the same, I'd sooner ship aboard one of the old steamers."

Once they got on board, Andrea was assigned to a tidy little cabin right next door to an identical one where Uncle Cyril and Jeff slept in the upper and lower bunks. However, the ship did not resemble the Love Boat that Andrea had been secretly hoping to see. A lot of people were travelling with babies and small children. Some of the passengers were very old. They weren't wearing evening clothes, just the usual jeans, shirts, and sneakers they wore at home. There were no waiters in white jackets. The captain wore a dark sweater with some unspectacular insignia on it. Supper was served in a small cafeteria. There wasn't any orchestra and there was no place to dance even if there had been music. Everybody went to bed early.

The next morning they reached Wilfred's Harbour. The harbour was large but the community itself was tiny. A semicircle of brightly painted houses was clustered on the rocky slopes at the foot of a high cliff.

The ship was soon moored beside the wharf, and within minutes the three of them made their way down the gangway, carrying their luggage and sleeping bags and the box of oranges and homemade bread that Aunt Pearl had insisted they take with them. Several mail bags and some cartons were unloaded, and within twenty minutes the ship was heading out to sea again.

After this rapid departure, Wilfred's Harbour was incredibly quiet. It took Andrea a few minutes to figure out why this was so. There were no cars or trucks anywhere; there wasn't even a street, just a broad pathway meandering around the houses. Apart from the chatter of some excited children who had come down to the wharf to watch the ship arrive and depart, the only persistent sound was the screeching of seagulls.

Mr. Spencer, whose boat Uncle Cyril was about to buy, was waiting on the wharf. The two men went off to arrange the transfer of ownership, leaving Andrea and Jeff sitting on their duffle bags to wait for them. The sun was shining and, for a change, it was warm enough to shed their jackets. Andrea felt relieved to be on dry land again.

"I wouldn't want to live in this place," she remarked, taking in her surroundings.

"Don't look too bad to me," Jeff observed.

"Well, it is pretty but there's no road and no cars. How do people get where they want to go?"

"They walk, sure. Or they travel in a boat," replied Jeff.

"Yeah, but what if they want to go to some bigger place — you know, like Toronto?"

"They get aboard the coast boat, just like we did. Then when they get upalong, they can take a bus or a train or a plane," he explained patiently. "But I don't say as many of 'em would want to go to Toronto. What would they do when they got there?"

"Oh, honestly!" sputtered Andrea. How could Jeff not think about all the things there were to do in Toronto? She was always telling him about the Royal Ontario Museum, where her whole class went to look at Chinese tombs and things, and the North York Sports Complex, where she went swimming in an Olympic-size pool, and the Eaton Centre, where you could buy absolutely anything you wanted if you just had enough money. And there were all those restaurants besides. Jeff listened to her politely but he didn't seem the least bit impressed.

For a long time Andrea and Jeff hardly exchanged a word. It was fulfilling just to sit there and soak up the warm sunshine and to eat some of the oranges. At last Uncle Cyril and Mr. Spencer returned. By this time they were chatting like old friends.

"My dear man, I'm sad to see her go but I got no choice. Fished all me life but I never seen the likes of this," Mr. Spencer was saying solemnly.

"Fish is some scarce," agreed Uncle Cyril.

"Foreign trawlers. I say that's the reason, sir," explained Mr. Spencer earnestly.

"Too many boats after too few cod fish and that's the truth," added Cyril.

"The way it is on this coast, we got them St. Pierre fishermen crossing the line besides. Who knows what they're up to in the dark of the night?" asked Mr. Spencer, suspicion in his voice.

" 'Tis hard to say," Cyril nodded.

"Seeing as I'm getting me pension now, I decided to retire," said Mr. Spencer. He stood on the wharf and looked down at his former boat and gave her a friendly salute as if he were saying goodbye to an old friend.

The boat was called *Blanche and Marilyn* and had the name painted in large white letters on the stern and on the bow. It now officially belonged to Cyril. He looked down proudly at the vessel. "Well, girl, what do you think of her?" he asked Andrea.

Andrea was disappointed. The boat wasn't very big. There was a deck over the forward section, a cabin in the middle, and the stern was wide open like a big row-boat. Built of wood, it was painted dark green on top, with the hull a muddy grey colour. The *Blanche and Marilyn* looked sturdy, but not very comfortable.

Uncle Cyril didn't wait for Andrea's reply. He climbed aboard and looked up at Jeff and Andrea from the deck. "All aboard, crew!" he commanded.

Jeff jumped down onto the deck right away, as enthusiastic as his father and just as intrigued by every-thing around him. Andrea lingered on the wharf, wishing the coast boat hadn't sailed away. It had been a lot nicer than this scruffy-looking fishing boat.

"Hey, c'm'ere, Andrea!" called Jeff. "Come and see your new quarters."

Andrea cautiously climbed down the ladder that had been built into the side of the wharf. From the bottom rung, she had to leap onto the deck of the boat, and she landed with a thud. She followed Jeff through the wheelhouse and down into the cabin, which was in the bow and looked about the size of a large doll's house. It was dark and smelled funny. She peered inside with a sense of dread.

"Is this the kitchen?" she asked, observing a row of battered saucepans hanging on hooks.

"The galley, sure," replied Jeff.

In the dim light from a single porthole, she could see a two-burner propane stove and a tiny little sink with a hand pump beside it. Above the sink was a cupboard holding plastic mugs and plates. In the middle of this cramped triangular room was a wooden table fastened to the floor. There were built-in benches on either side. It didn't look the least bit comfortable.

"Where does anybody sleep?" asked Andrea in alarm. The boat didn't seem to have any beds.

"Me and Dad sleeps on the settees," Jeff explained, pointing to the two benches. "You get the forepeak."

"The what?"

"The forepeak. Look here." He pointed towards a narrow, dark space right up in the bow. It wasn't high enough to stand up in but there was a bunk of sorts with room for one thin person. It was, Andrea noticed with relief, at least separated from the rest of the cabin by a plywood partition.

"You'll get used to it," said Jeff with the air of someone who understood everything there was to know about going to sea.

"Who do you suppose Blanche and Marilyn are?" Andrea wondered aloud.

"Most likely be Mr. Spencer's daughters. Or perhaps his wife and daughter. Some of his family, anyhow."

"How long do you think it will take to get to Anderson's Arm in . . . this?" Andrea asked warily.

"Jig time. Won't be more than two or three days, if we gets good weather," replied Jeff.

"That doesn't sound like jig time to me," stated Andrea flatly. She was beginning to wish she had stayed home with Aunt Pearl and Matthew.

"Um . . . Jeff . . . there's something I was wondering . . ."

"What?"

"Where does a person . . . go?"

"Go? Go where?"

"You know, stupid . . . go to the bathroom. Where's the bathroom?"

"No bathroom on board. This is a fishing boat. We just do it overboard." Jeff shrugged and then tried to suppress a laugh.

"Overboard!" gasped Andrea, horrified at the prospect.

"Aw don't fret. We'll find you a bucket someplace," Jeff reassured her. He started poking around in a locker full of odds and ends under the steps. He soon found a battered steel pail and handed it to Andrea.

"Thanks a whole lot," she said without gratitude.

"We'll make a sailor out of you yet," he grinned.

Just then Uncle Cyril appeared in the cabin doorway, clutching several bags of groceries in his arms.

He handed them to Andrea. "All right, cook, here's your first duty. Get those cans and jars stowed so they won't roll around if we gets a breeze. Best be quick, too. We got favourable weather today so we're getting underway right now."

With that, he returned to the wheelhouse and started the engine. Mr. Spencer untied the lines and tossed them aboard. He watched wistfully as the trim little vessel backed away from the wharf. With Cyril at the wheel, the boat headed for the narrow gap in the rocks that marked the exit from the peaceful, sheltered harbour. Andrea looked back to see Mr. Spencer and several children waving goodbye. Gradually, the tiny community of Wilfred's Harbour disappeared from view. Ahead lay the open ocean.

CHAPTER THREE

FOG. THEY HAD SEEN NOTHING BUT THICK, wet fog since leaving Wilfred's Harbour. When this journey began, Andrea had figured she would have all kinds of things to write her mother about, but what was there to say? For nearly two days they had been feeling their way along at a snail's pace. Fog and more fog. It was getting pretty boring but at least the sea was calm.

It was just as boring eating so many peanut butter sandwiches—until Uncle Cyril decided to try out his scallop-fishing gear. This was a bulky, complicated piece of equipment made of metal and nylon mesh. It hung over the stern of the boat and, when lowered into the sea by a powerful winch, it was towed slowly along the bottom of the ocean. When it was hauled back up, it could contain several bucketfuls of scallops. As it happened, the place where Cyril had tested his gear was not a particularly good fishing ground but they did catch enough for a meal for the three of them.

Cyril cut the scallops out of their shells and fried them in a pan over the little stove. After that they sat on deck in the fog and stuffed themselves. It wasn't the least bit like the last time Andrea had ordered scallops at The Twin Mermaids in Toronto. Then, there had been candles on the tables, checkered table-cloths, and fishing nets hanging from the ceiling holding an assortment of sea shells. Nevertheless, sitting here with the ocean all around them, the fresh scallops tasted better than anything Andrea had ever eaten in a restaurant.

Jeff picked up one of the empty shells and, curling his index finger around the edge, propelled it into the ocean sideways so that it skipped along the surface half a dozen times before it sank.

"Hey, don't do that," Andrea protested.

"Why not?"

"Because the shells are pretty. I want to keep them and put them around my room when I get back to Anderson's Arm."

Jeff and his father laughed. "There'll be plenty more where those came from," said Cyril, "but if you want them you can have them."

After dinner, Jeff took his turn steering the boat. They were proceeding very slowly because of the poor visibility. Every now and then, Cyril shut off the engine and they listened for the sound of fog-horns on the shore or bell-buoys on the ocean. If they heard anything, Cyril consulted a small book called the *Aid to Navigation*. It listed every fog-horn, bell-buoy, and light-house on the coasts of Newfoundland. Each horn had its own distinct sequence of sounds. It might be two short blasts and then one long one, or maybe four short ones in a row. This enabled mariners to know where they were in relation to the coast, even when they couldn't see it — like today.

Unfortunately Cyril had no navigational charts for that part of the coast. He explained to Andrea that a chart is a map of the ocean. There were several on board but they all described the shoreline to the *west* of Wilfred's Harbour. The *Blanche and Marilyn* was now heading east.

For the past several hours, they had heard only the gentle lapping of a quiet ocean, but they had seen something that thrilled Andrea. Through the mist she had suddenly seen a large, dark face with plaintive brown eyes looking right at her.

"Look!" she gasped, tugging Jeff's sleeve and pointing out at the hazy surface of the water.

Quickly the face disappeared below the water as silently as it had appeared.

"Only a seal, sure," Jeff observed nonchalantly.

"A seal! A real seal!" squealed Andrea.

"What's so special? There's t'ousands of 'em."

"I never saw one before. Well, yes, I did see one once in the aquarium at Niagara Falls. But I never saw one . . . just swimming around like that."

"You'll see plenty more," said Uncle Cyril. "Sons of guns eat more fish than I do these days."

"Dad, where do you think we're to?" asked Jeff a bit anxiously.

"I reckon we got to be somewhere south of the Burin Peninsula by now," said Cyril, stroking his chin.

"What if we're lost?" asked Andrea plaintively. She had never doubted Uncle Cyril's ability before. He had been going to sea all his life in one sort of ship or another. But all this fog — it made her wonder how safe they were.

"What if we run out of food?" she worried.

"Don't you fret, girl. We can always drag for scallops. Or we can head for shore and put into some outport and buy some grub," Cyril added reassuringly.

"But how will we find any places in the fog?"

"Fog don't last for ever. The wind will shift and blow it away," proclaimed Jeff, who was obviously enjoying being in charge of steering the boat.

Cyril had stopped the engine again and they were drifting silently.

"Listen," he said urgently. "Do you hear something?"

All three of them strained to listen. In a few seconds they heard it—a low-pitched, thudding sound.

"That's a vessel's engine, a pretty big one, too, and not far off," Cyril estimated. "Hope to heaven she's got her radar working and can see us."

They sat in alert silence, the baritone rumbling growing louder as some unseen ship drew nearer. Then they heard a change in pace—a slower vroom . . . vroom . . . vroom—indicating that the oncoming ship was slowing down.

Suddenly, out of the fog emerged the outline of another vessel very much larger than theirs. It was only a dozen metres away.

"Well, here's a bit of luck," smiled Cyril. "Now we can ask these fellows where we're to."

The vessels drifted closer to one another.

"Ahoy there, skipper," hollered Cyril. "Can you give us our position, please?

A man wearing a uniform was holding a loud hailer

as he stepped out on the wing of the bridge of the other vessel. His ship didn't have a name, only a number painted in very large figures on its side.

"Il est défendu de pêcher ici! Restez-là! Vous devez nous suivre! C'est un patrouilleur de la pêcherie."

"Thunderin' Jaysus!" exclaimed Cyril. "What in creation is this all about?"

"I think he's talkin' French, Dad," whispered Jeff, suddenly less sure of himself.

"I know it's French," said Andrea nervously.

"Can you understand him?" Jeff asked, surprised.

"What's he sayin'?" her uncle demanded urgently.

"He says it's a patrol boat and we're not allowed to fish here and that we have to follow him. Somewhere."

"What in the name of all that's holy for?" cried Cyril angrily. "We're not fishing!"

"Avez-vous compris?" called the uniformed man. *"Il faut que vous nous suiviez,* Blanche et Marilyn*!"* he repeated, pronouncing the name of the boat "Blonsh-ay-Maree-leen."

"He says we have to —" Andrea began.

"You tell him we're *not* fishing. Tell him we're not

sure of our position. This fella's making a mistake!"

"Well, I'll try," said Andrea, clearing her throat. *"Nous ne sommes pas pêcheurs,"* she yelled. *"Nous sommes perdus. Pouvez-vous me dire . . ."* She had to stop for a minute to try to think what to say. She didn't know how to ask for a navigational position in French. Her class had never studied that in French immersion.

"Ask him where we're to," repeated her uncle.

"Où sommes-nous, s'il vous plaît?" she shouted.

"Ce sont les lieux de pêche réservés pour les pêcheurs de pétoncle de St. Pierre et Miquelon. Il est interdit aux Canadiens de pêcher ici!"

"Mais nous ne pêchons pas! Nous sommes en route à Anderson's Arm," shouted Andrea in frustration.

The two vessels had now drifted so close together that the loud hailer was no longer needed. The first man was joined on deck by two other uniformed men. They ignored Andrea's explanations as they scanned the *Blanche and Marilyn*, pointing at the scallop-fishing gear at the stern of the boat.

"Mademoiselle," said the man who appeared to be in charge, *"ce n'est pas vrai. Voilà la preuve."* He was pointing to the small pile of scallop shells Andrea had saved to take home and decorate her room.

Andrea gasped. Were those few shells evidence of some terrible crime they had committed?

Her uncle spoke up again. "Now look here, we never fished them around here, me son. We fished them hours ago, back near Red Island in Newfoundland. A feed for our dinner is what it was. I just bought this boat and I'm ferrying her home where I got me licence to fish scallops."

It was no use. Apparently none of the uniformed men understood English. Andrea pleaded with them in French but they simply would not believe her. The scallop shells were right there on the deck in broad daylight. If only Andrea had let Jeff hurl them all into the ocean.

"Vous êtes en état d'arrestation, mon capitaine," said the captain of the other ship. *"Ne résistez pas!"*

"We're under arrest," sobbed Andrea.

"A fine kettle of fish this is," growled her uncle. "I guess we got no choice. We got to do what he says, for the time being, but don't you youngsters fret. We never broke any rules and we'll be clear of this lot in no time at all."

"Well, at least we're not lost any more," remarked Jeff, trying to put a bright face on the situation.

"Where are we? Where are they making us go?" asked Andrea, through her tears.

"St. Pierre. Can't be far," explained her uncle. "I knew it was close by but in this fog . . . well, I never stopped to think about their new regulations and all. Been lots of trouble about the fishing boundaries between them and Newfoundland this past while."

"I always wanted to see St. Pierre," said Jeff, "but not like this."

"What's so special about it?" Andrea asked.

"It's French. Foreign port," explained Cyril.

"You mean French, like Quebec?"

"No, no. girl. St. Pierre is altogether different. It's a

small group of islands hard by the coast of Newfoundland but they belong to France. Not exactly belong — more like they're a part of France, like a territory is in Canada. For hundreds of years, St. Pierre has been their fishing base on this side of the ocean. Nowadays, with fish so scarce, it seems the two governments have got the ocean hereabouts all carved up like it was a patch of potato gardens. No one is allowed to fish in the other fella's space."

"But how can they tell where the lines are?" asked Andrea. "The ocean all looks the same."

"It's all marked on the charts. What you do is get your position on the loran—that's a navigation machine. No problem to know where you're to. Trouble is, I don't have one but I'll buy one soon as I make a bit of money from scallops."

"I wonder if it's going to be like Paris?" Andrea wondered hopefully. She had read a lot of stories that took place in Paris.

"Don't say as it will. Likely be more like St. John's," speculated her uncle.

"I was thinking how it might be more like Gander. I know they got an airport there. An international airport," Jeff put in.

They were all wrong. It wasn't the least bit like any of those places. They followed the police boat for nearly an hour and finally emerged from the fog inside a broad harbour. In front of them stood a tidy town that was unlike anything they had ever seen. Andrea stared in fascination. Part of France, she thought. Now she really would have something to write her mother about.

Chapter Four

"Jail?" spluttered Cyril. "You got it all wrong, sir! I never fished so much as one scallop in your territory. I was only —"

"*Capitaine Baxter, on vous accuse d'avoir violé les traités de pêche entre la France et le Canada. Malheureusement, je n'ai pas le choix. Il faut que vous restiez ici jusqu'au moment où on entendra votre cause,*" pronounced the stern-looking police officer from behind his wide desk. He wore the same kind of uniform the men in the patrol boat had worn.

"What's he sayin' now?" Cyril asked Andrea, who looked back at him with tears in her eyes.

"There's some treaty. He says . . . you broke the law. And you have to go to jail," she gulped, hardly able to tell him, "until your case can be heard in court!"

"Jumpins, Dad! That might take months!" blurted Jeff, who was close to tears as well.

"Now look here," Cyril demanded of the officer. "Surely I got the right to call the Canadian Fisheries people over in St. John's. Someone there will get me out of this mess."

Andrea translated, and the police officer sighed and crossed his arms across his broad chest. "*Eh bien! . . .*" he muttered, a flicker of a smile crossing his face. Somewhat grudgingly, he shoved his telephone across the desk so that Cyril could reach it.

Cyril was able to reach a telephone operator in Newfoundland who connected him to the Department of Fisheries. The distant phone rang and rang. Finally, a recorded announcement asked callers to leave their number and told them that their call would be returned. It didn't say when. "Why in the name of Old Harry don't they answer the phone in person?" grumbled Cyril with growing impatience.

"Maybe they're closed today," suggested Jeff.

"What day is this?" asked Cyril.

"I'm pretty sure it's Saturday," Andrea replied.

While they had been travelling, they had lost track of the time. On board a ship, one day seemed very much like another.

"I'm some vexed," said Cyril wearily. "That means we got to wait till Monday."

"You know something?" Andrea said quietly, not wanting to add to her uncle's troubles. "Monday's a holiday. It's Canada Day—July the first."

"Lord love us! They won't be at work Monday neither," sighed Cyril. He turned to the officer who was waiting patiently and in a slow, polite voice said, "Now then, sir, you can put me in your jail if that's what you got a mind to do but what about these youngsters here?" He pointed at Jeff and Andrea. "You can't go putting them in prison. They got nothing to do with this. They're innocent, you hear me? Innocent!"

"Ah, oui, les jeunes," nodded the officer, who now seemed to have grasped what Cyril was saying to him. After all, the word "innocent" was the same in both languages, even if it was pronounced differently. He looked at Jeff and Andrea with friendly concern and

asked, *"Vos enfants, capitaine?"*

Andrea explained her family relationship to the police officer. *"Jeff est son fils. C'est mon oncle, le frère de mon père. Mon père est mort."*

"I just remembered something," interrupted Cyril. "We got some family over here. On Pearl's side. Her mother's sister—Henrietta was her name—she came over here many long years ago to take a job in a hotel. Married a local fellow and raised a big family before she finally passed on. Now then, if I can just remember the name of the man she married . . . let me see . . . I believe his last name was Rowe or Roo or some such name as that."

"Qu'est-ce qui se passe?" enquired the policeman, wondering what they were talking about.

"Il est possible que nous ayons des cousins ici," explained Andrea. *"Leur nom de famille est Roo ou quelque chose comme ça."*

"Roux? La famille Roux, peut-être?" suggested the officer helpfully.

"Peut-être," nodded Andrea. *"Henriette était la tante de ma tante."*

The officer reached for a St. Pierre telephone directory and leafed through it until he came to a page on which there were three listings for the last name of Roux. He explained to Andrea that he would start calling and enquire about anyone who was descended from a former Newfoundlander named Henriette.

"Uncle Cyril, what's going to happen to us?" whispered Andrea, while the police officer talked rapidly to one person after another on his telephone.

"Don't you fret. This has all been a mistake and we'll be out of here before you knows it. Let's just hope, seein' as how we got some cousins here, there might be someone you and Jeff could stay with. Only a day or two. Won't be long," he said reassuringly.

"But what if there aren't any relatives? What if they all moved away or died or something?" asked Jeff anxiously.

"Don't seem too likely," concluded Cyril. "What I heard was Henrietta had a dozen youngsters."

"Bonnes nouvelles!" exclaimed the policeman with a smile, putting down the receiver. He told Andrea that he had located a woman who was a daughter of Henriette Roux and had explained the situation to her. Madame Cécile Foliot was a widow who rented rooms to tourists. She was coming to the police station right away.

Madame Foliot soon arrived, driving a sea-green Renault. She was a large woman whose dark hair was streaked with grey. She wore black slacks and a black blouse, gold earrings, and grey shoes. Her finger-nails were painted bright fuchsia.

"Ah, les pauvrets," she cried sympathetically the moment she caught sight of Andrea and Jeff. They were both so nervous by then they could barely manage to smile. *"Quel dommage!"* she murmured.

"Dites au revoir à votre père maintenant," ordered the policeman.

"C'est mon oncle," Andrea corrected him. "Goodbye, Uncle Cyril. I hope it's going to be okay where you're going," she added solemnly, trying to keep her voice from faltering.

"S'long, Dad," said Jeff bravely. "I hope you won't be there very long."

"I'll be all right, never you fear. Now then, you be sure to help this good woman all you can. She's your long-lost cousin. Jeff, you phone your mother soon as you can but don't go getting her all riled. Just tell her we're in St. Pierre. Tell her we'll be home soon," said Cyril firmly as the police officer ushered him down a corridor and through a door that slammed ominously shut behind them.

The three of them watched him go, then they walked out to Madame Foliot's car. Andrea and Jeff sat in silence as she drove them through the maze of narrow streets. The cars and trucks didn't look the same as they did at home. Most of them were French. The surrounding landscape looked a lot like it did in Anderson's Arm, with big, rocky hills, but the houses were quite different. Most of them were two stories high and some had three floors. They had been built very close together and quite near the street. Nobody had a front lawn. There weren't very many trees and none was any taller than a house.

There seemed to be dozens of small shops and most of them were located on street corners. Andrea wondered what was sold in them. She had so many questions. Just how long would they have to stay with Madame Foliot? What if Uncle Cyril was in serious trouble? What were they going to tell Aunt Pearl? What would her mother say, far away in Africa? She hoped her mother wouldn't hear about it until long after it was all over. With any luck, that would be soon.

"Faites comme chez vous!" chirped Madame Foliot cheerfully as she led Andrea and Jeff up a flight of stairs and showed each of them to their rooms. It was a big house with a lot of bedrooms. There was a sign outside that read "Auberge Cécile."

Andrea had gathered up all her belongings from the *Blanche and Marilyn* and stuffed them in her duffle bag. She now dropped it on the floor and sat down on the edge of the bed. She caught sight of her reflection in the bedroom mirror and realized she looked a real mess. No wonder Madame had called them poor little things. After all the travelling, and then living on her uncle's boat, her clothes were getting dirty. Her hair needed washing. Something dark and greasy—engine oil, maybe—had spilled on one of her white sneakers. She hoped that Madame Foliot had a washing machine. She had noticed that there was a big, old-fashioned tub in the bathroom down the hall. She would ask Madame if she could take a bath this evening. After a while her thoughts drifted back to Uncle Cyril.

What must it be like where he was, and how was he going to manage since he didn't speak French?

She walked over to the window, brushed the curtain aside, and just stared out at nothing in particular for a long time. There was a small garden below her, enclosed by a fence. Someone had planted rows of something— vegetables maybe—but so far only small green plants were showing. An orange cat was sitting on the fence. It was beginning to rain. A tear ran down Andrea's cheek. "What am I doing here?" she asked herself. "What are we going to do?"

"A table! Dépêchez-vous, mes enfants," called Madame from the bottom of the stairs.

Andrea snapped out of her dark mood and went to look for Jeff.

"There's food," she told him. "Let's go."

Jeff looked just as depressed as she had been. He had been lying on his bed staring at the ceiling but he got up and followed Andrea downstairs.

There was a big, oval-shaped table in the dining-room. A teen-aged boy with curly, dark brown hair was already sitting down. He wore a black sweatshirt with paint splattered on one sleeve. He was, they learned, Madame Foliot's son, and his name was Philippe.

"Mon bébé" was the way she introduced him, which Andrea thought was really kind of silly because he was no baby. It turned out that he was seventeen and the youngest of a family of five, the rest of whom had married and moved away.

"Bonjour," said Andrea politely.

Jeff didn't say anything and just sat with a forlorn expression on his face.

"Ton frère ne parle pas français?" asked Philippe, after they had begun to eat.

"C'est mon cousin. Je n'ai pas de frère. Il parle un petit peu," she said, looking at Jeff hopefully. She knew he studied French at school but was too shy to say anything.

Jeff was picking at his food. It didn't taste like the food he was used to at home. They had been served some kind of stew which Madame described as "ragoût." Jeff wasn't sure he liked it. Luckily, there was a basket full of bread on the table and he ate as much of that as he could without appearing too greedy. There was rhubarb pie for dessert and that was really, really good. When Jeff was offered a second helping, he smiled for the first time since he had arrived in St. Pierre et Miquelon.

When dinner was over, Andrea knew they couldn't postpone phoning Aunt Pearl any longer. Jeff didn't want to place the call in case he encountered a French-speaking operator, so Andrea volunteered to do it. She still wasn't sure what to say.

"Hello, Aunt Pearl. It's me," Andrea began carefully.

"I'm some glad to hear your voice, my dear. Not hearing from you for a nice while, I was a little worried," replied Pearl. "Where are you to?"

"Umm, you remember your aunt?"

"Aunt? Which aunt?"

"Your Aunt Henrietta. You know, the one who went to St. Pierre and got married? Way back when?"

"Yes, I remember all right," answered Pearl, sounding puzzled. "What's that got to do with anything? Poor soul is dead and gone now."

"Umm, well, we're here visiting with her daughter."

There was a brief silence as Aunt Pearl tried to absorb this astonishing information. "You mean to tell me you're in St. Pierre? And you're visiting Henrietta's daughter?" she asked in amazement. "I never knew Cyril was planning to go there."

"Well, we didn't really plan to, but . . ."

"And which daughter would that be?"

"Her name is Cécile. Cécile Foliot."

"Yes, I recall there was a Cécile. And a Marie. And Annette . . . and Yvonne and . . . well, there was quite a crowd of them. How on earth did you find her?"

"We had some help."

"We lost track of Henrietta's family over the years, seeing as they lived so far away. I'm surprised Cyril even remembered Henrietta's name. Can I have a word with him now?" asked Pearl.

"Ah . . . well . . . he's not here right now," she faltered. "But Jeff is. I'll put him on."

"Hi, Mom."

"How you getting on, Jeffie, my son?"

"Okay, I guess. I wish I was home."

"Hurry on home then."

"We can't. Not until Dad gets out of jail."

"Jail!" exploded Pearl.

"It's all a big mistake," Jeff began. "You see, we got lost in the fog. And then this police boat arrived. They said we were fishing in their territory. And we weren't fishing at all. They made us come here. And they put Dad in jail. So me and Andrea are staying here with these cousins."

"Angels and saints!" exclaimed Pearl, in a state of shock. "Jeffie, could you let me have a word with Cécile?"

"No, I don't think so, Mom. She only talks French," he explained.

"And I only talk English," sighed Pearl.

"Aunt Pearl, it's me again," said Andrea, grabbing the phone from Jeff. "I can speak to her. She seems really nice. She's got this big house, and the food is pretty good, and we're all right, so don't worry about us. You see, the trouble was that when Uncle Cyril tried to phone the Canadian Fisheries people no one was there because this is a long weekend. That's why he's in jail. He's innocent but he couldn't get anyone to help him."

"We'll just see about that!" said Pearl with determination. "I'll get hold of one of those bloody paper pushers if it's the last thing I do!"

"I sure hope so," said Andrea plaintively. "Will you call us back? The number is 508 41.55.55."

"You'll be hearing from me. And soon!" cried Pearl as she wrote down the number and then hung up the phone.

CHAPTER FIVE

ANDREA AWOKE ON SUNDAY MORNING AND heard the distant clanging of a church bell. It took her a few seconds to realize where she was and to remember the alarming events of the previous day. The rain had stopped falling and sunshine was filtering into the bedroom beneath the green window blind. She got up, raised the blind, and looked out. The sky was clear blue and the distant ocean was as dark as ink. The tidy town of St. Pierre looked quite different today, with all the brightly painted houses resembling a multi-coloured quilt. Andrea noticed a blue, white, and red flag flying from the top of a building.

"I'm in France," she thought. "This is St. Pierre but it's also France." For the first time, she felt a little bit of excitement about being here.

Andrea and Jeff arrived downstairs for breakfast just as Madame Foliot was leaving for church. Philippe was already at the table so they joined him. Breakfast consisted of bread and butter and jam. There was nothing else except coffee, which neither Andrea nor Jeff liked. Apparently the Foliot family didn't eat cornflakes, or Sugar Pops, or anything like that. There were no muffins and no eggs, either. Just long, skinny, warm loaves of bread.

"Some good," said Jeff with his mouth full. "This bread's not store-bought. It's homemade, like Mom makes sometimes." He reached for more.

"Holy Moley. Philippe's mother must have got up awfully early to bake it," Andrea remarked, feeling a bit guilty that she hadn't been on hand to help this woman who was being so kind to them.

"Elle l'a acheté à la boulangerie," Philippe interjected, then he pronounced, slowly and carefully in English, "at . . . the . . . bakery."

Andrea looked across at him in surprise. "We didn't know you could speak English, Philippe," she said.

"A little," he grinned. "I study it at school."

"And I study French! I'm in French immersion. Or, at least, I was. I'm really from Toronto but right now my mom's away so I'm staying in Anderson's Arm. That's in Newfoundland."

"I have been to Newfoundland," said Philippe.

"Whereabouts?" asked Jeff.

"Burin and Grand Bank and St. Lawrence. I play soccer. Sometimes we go there. Sometimes they go here," he explained.

"Come here," Andrea corrected him politely.

"Bet that's good fun," added Jeff.

"Fun? Yes," agreed Philippe. "Do you like fun? Today perhaps? It is Sunday and I do not work."

"Umm, what kind of fun?" asked Andrea cautiously. "We don't have to play soccer, do we?"

Philippe laughed. Andrea could see his strong white teeth. One of them had a gold cap on it. He was actually quite cute looking. "Not soccer. Today we can make fun to see St. Pierre. It is something new for you, no?"

"Well, yes, it is," Andrea replied. "I suppose we

could see some more of it. We're not doing anything special."

"Nothing special at all," added Jeff.

"Laissez-moi vous piloter," offered Philippe.

Andrea washed the few breakfast dishes and then the three of them set off down the road while Philippe explained that he had a summer job as a painter. He and several other students were painting the rooms in the high school. When that was finished, they were going to paint the rooms in the elementary school.

"Jeez, b'y, you got stuck with school the whole year long," Jeff said sympathetically.

"This is different. For this I receive money," Philippe explained proudly, as he led Jeff and Andrea past the school so they could look in the window and admire the fresh coat of cream-coloured paint.

All roads in St. Pierre seemed to lead to the harbour. Soon they were walking across the public square beyond which were several wharves crowded with ships. Most of them were fishing vessels—big, rusty, deep-sea draggers that looked as if they had survived a lot of bad weather. Some were French but several were flying flags Andrea and Jeff did not recognize and they had strange names painted on their sterns.

"Espagnol," said Philippe, pointing to a large dragger. The home port painted on the stern was Bilbao, a city in Spain. "They arrive here for fuel and supplies. Sometimes because of big . . . ah . . . big . . . *orages*," Philippe tried to explain, groping for the right word.

"Storms," said Andrea helpfully.

"*Oui*. When big storms arrive on Le Grand Banks, many ships come here," Philippe concluded.

"They must be catching t'ousands of fish," remarked Jeff, who was impressed with the size of the draggers.

"More like millions or trillions," countered Andrea.

"True enough, t'ousands," agreed Jeff.

"Oh, Lord," thought Andrea as she remembered that "thousands" in Newfoundland didn't mean precisely that. It meant an enormous quantity of whatever they were describing. It was tricky enough trying to help Philippe along with his English, but every once in a while Jeff would use a word she had to translate, too.

"And they shouldn't be taking so many of 'em. Dad says the trouble is too many foreign fishing boats are out there and that's why the cod stocks are going down, and he says—"

"Oh, look! There's the *Blanche and Marilyn*!" Andrea sang out, rapidly trying to change the subject. Jeff didn't seem to realize that in *this* place, he and Andrea were the foreigners. This was no time to start criticizing anybody.

"That's Dad's boat! Right there," cried Jeff, pointing it out to Philippe, who stared at their unoccupied boat, which looked rather sad and lonely tied to one of the docks. "And we'll be going home in her soon."

Following another road that led up a hill to the edge of town, they came to a large cemetery. Rows of crosses ended at a cliff above the sea. The graves were very close to one another. Andrea and Jeff were surprised to see that the coffins were above the surface of the ground, boxed in concrete.

"This graveyard is weird," Andrea observed. "Everywhere else they bury dead people *under* the ground."

"Rocks," Philippe tried to explain. "Too much rocks." He pointed at the surroundings, which were mainly solid rock with only a thin layer of moss or grass.

"Too *many* rocks," Andrea couldn't help saying, thinking to herself that Philippe still had a way to go with his English.

Philippe shrugged. "Come. *Mon grand-père et ma grand-mère.*" He led the way through the maze of graves. At the far end of the cemetery stood a pair of crosses side by side at the head of two cement tombs. One bore the inscription "Louis Philippe Roux 1908-1981." The other read "Henriette Ethel Roux 1910-1990."

"That must be my mom's aunt," noted Jeff solemnly, "but look at that. They spelled her name wrong. It should be Henrietta with an 'a'."

"That's the French way, stupid," proclaimed Andrea righteously. "She probably changed the way she spelled it once she decided she was going to stay here."

"She never changed the way she spelled her middle name," observed Jeff.

Andrea thought for a moment. "I don't think there is a French way to spell Ethel."

"Anyhow, this place gives me the creeps. It's probably full of ghosts." Jeff shivered as a cold breeze from the ocean swirled around them.

"I kind of like it here," said Andrea dreamily. "I like places with ghosts."

"I don't. I want to get going," said Jeff impatiently.

"*Alors*, we go to the café now for a . . . *petit coup*," directed Philippe.

"Right!" beamed Andrea.

"For a what?" Jeff asked Andrea warily. "What kinda stuff do we get at the café?"

"*Un petit coup!*" teased Andrea. "Hah! I won't tell you. It's a surprise."

As they entered Aux Marins, a little café in the centre of town, Jeff was apprehensive. He didn't like strange food or drinks. In fact, he didn't like restaurants at all, except for the burger place in Gander where his family sometimes ate when they went to town to shop.

Philippe ordered a Coke. Andrea decided she would have one, too. Jeff ordered a Pepsi, relieved to find a familiar beverage in this odd place.

The café was rather dark inside and looked more like a bar, which it also was. It was the sort of place that would certainly have been off-limits for a girl of Andrea's age back home. Over by the window, a young couple sat staring dreamily into each other's eyes as they sipped red wine. At the counter, a man wearing rubber boots and sea-going clothes was quaffing something amber-coloured from a very small glass as he chatted with another man who was drinking beer.

There were tables and chairs on the sidewalk just outside the front door so Andrea suggested that they sit at one of them. She sipped her Coke slowly and looked around. The café overlooked the harbour and the *Place du Général de Gaulle*, which was the centre of town. Philippe told them that it was named in honour of the leader of the Free French in World War II. In the middle of the *Place* were bright flower beds and, surrounding them, benches where older people were sitting and chatting. Off to one side several men, dressed in their Sunday best, were playing some kind of game—rolling big metal balls against one another.

Even though the shops were closed, this was a busy

place. The three of them sat and watched as the passenger ferry made its daily departure for Newfoundland. A fat man walked by, pulled by a Labrador dog on a leash. A young mother pushing a dark blue baby carriage trotted past them. Three boys on bicycles pedalled by in a great hurry to get somewhere. All the while, a parade of Renaults and Peugeots zoomed along the road that encircled *Place du Général de Gaulle*. Andrea remembered the only place you could go for refreshments in Anderson's Arm was a chip truck parked near the wharf. In contrast, this was so . . . well, so French. She decided then and there that she liked it.

While they were having their drinks, they heard the sound of an airplane. The airport, across the harbour, was visible from where they sat. They watched as a twin-engined plane circled the town before descending.

Philippe glanced at his wrist-watch. "Air St. Pierre, from Halifax. Many people come to St. Pierre now. From Canada. From United States. From everywhere. Tourists —they like St. Pierre in summer."

"Well, I can see it is sort of special," agreed Andrea. "It's too bad we have to leave right away—just as soon as my uncle gets out of jail."

"Could we go and visit him?" asked Jeff. He had downed his Pepsi and now was anxious to leave.

"Alas, not possible," replied Philippe, shaking his head. "Those *gendarmes* . . . they are . . . how do you say . . .?"

"Strict?" suggested Andrea.

"*Oui*. They are not *St. Pierrais*. They are sent from France. Sometimes they are not happy to come here."

"That's no big surprise," muttered Jeff, who didn't share Andrea's growing interest in this place. He was beginning to feel he had been exiled here himself.

"They say it is . . . *rustique*. Also it is cold . . . too cold," Philippe continued.

Andrea didn't say anything. She didn't want to hurt Philippe's feelings but it really *was* pretty cold for the end of June. She was glad she had brought along her black leather jacket and a turtle-neck shirt.

"*Ah, mon Dieu. J'ai oublié quelque chose!*" exclaimed Philippe, abruptly jumping up and yanking his wallet out of his pocket to pay for their drinks.

"*Qu'est-ce que c'est?*" asked Andrea, wondering what it was he had forgotten.

"*Cet avion* . . . I forget. Two people arrive on this airplane to stay at Auberge Cécile. Tourists. No, not tourists —scientists. I have promise to be at home to help my mother to understand. They do not speak French."

"You're the translator?" Andrea smiled quizzically.

"Yes," admitted Philippe, who began to laugh so that you could see his perfect teeth and the one with the gold cap. "Not good maybe, but I try," he apologized.

"I'll help you, if you like," Andrea volunteered shyly.

"*Bonne*. Okay," smiled Philippe, and they hurried out of the café. "*A qui arrivera le premier!*" he challenged.

And the three of them ran all the way back to Auberge Cécile.

CHAPTER SIX

A MAN AND A WOMAN WERE HAULING luggage out of a Citroen taxi as Andrea, Jeff, and Philippe arrived, somewhat breathlessly, at the front door of Auberge Cécile.

Madame Foliot was standing in the doorway to greet her two new guests. *"Bonjour!"* she cried vigorously. *"Nous sommes enchantés de vous avoir chez nous!"*

"Hello there," replied the man. "I'm Tom Horwood and this is Karen Corkum, my wife. What a lovely day."

"Philippe, apporte les bagages tout de suite, s'il te plaît," requested Madame, pointing at the growing mountain of duffle bags, brief-cases, and mysterious-looking crates and boxes that kept emerging from the back of the small taxi. *"Vous avez la chambre numéro cinq, en haut. Faites comme chez vous,"* she welcomed.

"Did you catch that?" whispered Dr. Horwood to his wife.

She shook her head.

"Maybe I can help you," Andrea offered. "Your room is number five. If you follow me, I'll show you where everything is."

"Well, now, here's a young lady who really knows how to speak English," said Dr. Horwood, much relieved. "And what would your name be?"

"My name is Andrea. Of course I speak English. You see, I'm really from —"

"Now that is something I do admire," interrupted

Karen Corkum enthusiastically, "a kid who's at home in both languages."

"So, Andrea," said her husband, "if you're not too busy, maybe you'd be kind enough to stick around for a bit, until we get organized here. We're heading off to do some studies on Miquelon for the summer and we have to make a lot of arrangements . . . buy supplies, hire a boat, make phone calls, that kind of thing."

"Sure, no problem," smiled Andrea.

At noon, Madame placed a bowl as big as a bird bath full of steaming soup in the middle of the dining-room table. She asked Andrea to ladle it out to the other guests.

During the meal, the new arrivals mentioned that they had been married for less than a year and were both marine biologists. Tom Horwood was engaged in research at the marine laboratory in St. Andrew's, New Brunswick. Karen Corkum was a lecturer at Dalhousie University in Halifax. In the course of the school year, they could be together only on weekends, which was one of their prime reasons for working on a combined project this summer. They were going to do a field study of the Grey seal.

Andrea did her best to explain all this to Cécile Foliot and to Philippe, who both listened with keen interest.

Jeff was listening, too, and after a while he asked, "What kind of guns have you got?"

"Guns?" repeated Dr. Corkum.

"Right, guns. See, I was just wondering, well, how are you going to kill those seals?"

"Kill them? Ewww! That's disgusting," Andrea protested.

"No, no, no!" answered Dr. Horwood emphatically. "We didn't come here to kill anything. We're here to study living seals. We want to learn more about where they go, what they eat, how they look after their young —not how they die."

Jeff considered what they had said and then declared, "My dad says there are too many seals. They eat all the fish and that's the reason . . . well, part of the reason fishermen can't catch enough fish to make a living these days."

The two biologists exchanged glances, then Dr. Horwood cleared his throat. "Ahem. Well, there are differences of opinion on the question of whether seals are bad for the commercial fishery. That's one of the main reasons we're here—to help find some answers to that question. We intend to carry out an intensive study of the Grey seal in the great lagoon up on Miquelon. We plan to —"

The telephone rang.

Philippe got up to answer it. His mother and Andrea began to clear the table. *"C'est pour toi,"* he called to Andrea.

It was Aunt Pearl.

Andrea listened silently for what seemed to the others like a long time, then she exclaimed, "No kidding!" After another moment she said, "Wow!" Another silence lapsed before she cried, "That's brilliant!"

"What's happening? Lemme talk to Mom! Lemme talk!" Jeff pestered.

Andrea ended the phone conversation with a firm "Okay, okay. We'll get there! Goodbye," and then hung up. "Jeff, she says to give you a hug from her, but she had to hang up because she was waiting for an important call. Wait till I tell you! It looks like all hell's breaking loose."

"Goodness, what's going on?" enquired Dr. Horwood.

"Qu'est-ce qui se passe?" asked Cécile.

"That was my Aunt Pearl," Andrea began.

"Ah! Ma cousine!" said Madame Foliot brightly.

"I'll try and explain. It seems Aunt Pearl has been talking to, well, just about everybody. The minister of Fisheries, the premier of Newfoundland, some guy from . . . oh, I forget . . . foreign something."

"Foreign Affairs?" suggested Karen Corkum.

"I think so. Anyway, the day after tomorrow a bunch of them are coming here. And Aunt Pearl is coming, too . . . on the plane from St. John's! She wants us to be there to meet her at the airport."

"Mom's never flown in an airplane before!" exclaimed Jeff.

"Well, she will soon. And the government people all agree it's been a real fiasco, and Uncle Cyril never should have been put in jail, and they're going to get him out of there fast. And, oh, I nearly forgot—Aunt Pearl needs somewhere to stay." Andrea turned to

Madame Foliot. *"Ma tante a besoin d'une chambre. Est-ce qu'elle peut rester ici?"*

"Bien sûr!" said Cécile, smiling, *"Ce n'est pas la place qui manque, c'est ma cousine!"* she exclaimed, raising her hands in a dramatic gesture, pleased at the chance of meeting a distant relative she had never expected to see.

"Do I read this correctly?" asked Tom Horwood, who was trying to catch the drift of the conversation. "These women are cousins but they've never met?"

"Right. Their mothers were sisters. In Newfoundland. A long, long time ago."

"And, uh, somebody's in jail?" enquired Dr. Corkum tactfully.

"Yeah, my dad," replied Jeff, "but he's not supposed to be there at all. It's been a big mistake. Just wait. He'll be outta there quick as a wink."

Monday was Canada Day—in Canada—but in St. Pierre it was just an ordinary day when life went along as usual. Philippe went back to work painting the school. Jeff volunteered to go with him and help. He was getting fidgety just hanging around.

Andrea, on the other hand, was very busy. The scientists kept her occupied all day. First they had to go to the bank. Next they rented a post-box. Then they looked for a boat to hire to take them to the island of Miquelon. That wasn't a problem since there were all kinds of small fishing vessels not being used because of the fish shortage. After that they bought a boat-load of food since they were going to be camping for several weeks far from any store.

When they finally got all their supplies organized, Karen Corkum (she had asked Andrea to call her Karen) suggested that the two of them go shopping for perfume. St. Pierre, she explained, was famous as a source of French perfume at bargain prices.

"Mmmm. Mmmm! Try this," she suggested as she sprayed some Chanel No. 19 on her wrist. They were sitting side by side on a pair of stools at the counter in a small shop called Topaze. Twenty or thirty bottles of perfume stood in front of them. They all smelled wonderful. With the day's work behind them, their biggest concern now was trying to decide which of the many scents they liked the best.

"What's your favourite?" Karen asked Andrea.

"Miss Dior, I think. But . . ."

"But what?"

"I don't have any money. I can't afford to buy it," Andrea acknowledged sadly.

"Well, you do have *some* money," Karen smiled. She was quite pretty in a thin sort of way, Andrea thought. "You've got the money you earned today helping us."

"Oh!" said Andrea, brightening, not having realized she was going to be paid.

"So go ahead and choose some perfume. And why not buy some for your mother in Newfoundland, too?"

"My mom's not in Newfoundland; she's in Africa. I won't be seeing her . . . well, not for a long time,"

Andrea explained, suddenly feeling a pang of sadness. It really would be a long time.

"In Africa?" asked a puzzled Karen. "I thought someone said you lived in Anderson's Arm, Newfoundland."

"Yes, I do, but only till January. I really live in Toronto. My mom got this job teaching school in Africa, so I had to come here—well, not here, but to Newfoundland to stay with my aunt and uncle. Then my uncle went to collect his new fishing boat and, oh—it's a long story," Andrea sighed. At the moment, her life wasn't simple at all.

"My goodness," commented Karen sympathetically.

"It's not so bad. I kind of like travelling around. And St. Pierre is really okay. I wouldn't mind staying here for a bit longer . . . if only my uncle wasn't in jail."

CHAPTER SEVEN

ON TUESDAY MORNING, THE FOG RETURNED. When Andrea awoke, she could hear a fog-horn bleating hoarsely from a distant rock far out in the bay. She ran up the window blind but couldn't see further than the back yard, where the orange cat was once again sitting on the fence.

"What if the plane can't land?" asked Jeff anxiously, as they were eating their bread and jam at breakfast. "It's thick as soup out there."

"They've got radar and all that stuff. They'll get in," said Andrea reassuringly.

"I bet Mom is scared to death right now."

Near noon the fog lifted a little, and by two o'clock there was just enough visibility for the flight from St. John's to land on the single runway of St. Pierre's small airport.

The first passengers to leave the plane were two men dressed in dark business suits. Both of them were carry-ing brief-cases. Right behind them came Aunt Pearl, wearing a beige raincoat over her best summer dress, which usually she wore only to church. She looked anx-iously around for a familiar face.

"Mom! Mom!" Jeff called.

"Here we are!" shouted Andrea.

The three of them collided at the door that led from the customs and immigration counter into the main terminal. Pearl hugged them both and then burst into tears.

"Oh, my dears," she said between sobs, "I been some worried about you and Cyril."

"Don't worry," comforted Andrea. "People here have been very kind to us. I'm sure everything will turn out right."

"I'm some glad to see you, I can tell you that," Pearl said, pulling herself together. She took off her glasses and fished in her handbag for a handkerchief. "Now then, these two gentlemen—this one is Mr. Snow and this one's Mr. O'Leary—they're from the government, and they're going to get Cyril out of that prison."

Soon the five of them were crowded into a taxi headed for the Préfecture, the government administrative building, where they were met in the entrance hall by the same *gendarme* who had put Uncle Cyril in jail the previous Saturday.

"Bonjour, mes enfants!" he greeted Andrea and Jeff cheerfully. *"Vous êtes-vous bien amusés ici à St. Pierre?"*

"Oui, merci," answered Andrea politely.

"What did he say?" whispered Aunt Pearl.

"He was asking if we had been enjoying ourselves here," Andrea translated.

"Tell him I wants to go home to Newfoundland."

"Shh, Jeff. He did the best he could for us," Andrea scolded.

"I guess so, but I still wants outta here."

Mr. Snow and Mr. O'Leary were ushered into an office occupied by an important-looking man who had grey hair and was wearing a dark grey suit. Then the office door was shut, leaving Aunt Pearl, Andrea, and

Jeff to wait anxiously out in the hall. They sat down on a wooden bench. No one wanted to say what they were all thinking: what if these men couldn't get Uncle Cyril out of jail after all? They were in a foreign country now; the rules were different. Finally, Andrea broke the apprehensive silence.

"How did you like flying, Aunt Pearl?" she asked, with a grin.

"To tell the truth, it wasn't too bad at all. Gets you where you're going in a hurry. And they gave me a glass of ginger ale besides."

"Mom, where's Matt?" asked Jeff, who hadn't had time to think about his younger brother in the midst of all the excitement.

"Matt is staying over with the Noseworthys," she replied, just as the office door opened.

"Madame Bax-tair," said the man with the grey hair and the grey suit, *"j'espère que vous pourrez pardonner cet incident fâcheux. Votre mari sera ici aussitôt que possible."*

Pearl Baxter stared at him uncomprehendingly.

"It's okay, Aunt Pearl," whispered Andrea. "He says Uncle Cyril will be here right away."

It was true. In a few minutes, another door opened and through it strode Cyril Baxter, smiling from ear to ear. Pearl and the kids darted forward and hugged him. The *gendarme* smiled. Mr. Snow and Mr. O'Leary smiled. The man in the grey suit, who was the chief administrator of the French territory of St. Pierre and Miquelon, smiled too.

Everyone shook hands. It had all been a dreadful

mistake. There was no real evidence that Cyril had been fishing in forbidden waters. He had been telling the police the truth. He should never have been arrested. After apologizing, the chief administrator insisted on paying the cost of Aunt Pearl's airplane ticket.

"I got to admit," confided Cyril once the family was inside a taxi heading for Auberge Cécile, "it wasn't altogether bad. The bed was some hard but the place was clean and they gave me all the homemade bread I could eat for me breakfast. What do you think of that?"

"I think it came from the bakery," said Andrea knowingly.

"Only torment was the other fella in there. He was some drunk. He moaned and hollered the whole of the first night and I never got a wink of sleep. But in the morning they sent him home, and after that I was on me own and the place was as quiet as a church bell on Monday. By and by, they got me a radio so's I could hear a station over in Newfoundland, and last night some fella came by with a bunch of French picture magazines to look at."

That evening, Madame Foliot gave a party. Not only were they celebrating Cyril's release from jail but also the occasion when Cécile and Pearl, who shared the same grandmother, had finally met one another. These two cousins had something of a communication problem, of course, and Andrea had to work overtime translating for them while Cécile turned over the dusty pages of an old photograph album.

"Voilà ma mère, ma grand-mère, et ma tante il y a longtemps," said Cécile Foliot, pointing to a photograph of a smiling woman standing between two young girls wearing old-fashioned clothes. The black-and-white photograph was small and slightly out of focus.

"Look at that now!" repeated Aunt Pearl. "That's my mother standing beside my grandmother and my aunt, all those years ago. Look at this, Jeffie, my son. There's your great-grandmother when she was a young woman and your grandmother when she was a girl."

Jeff glanced at the faded photograph but wasn't particularly interested. He was engrossed in listening to the conversation his father was having with the two scientists. They planned to leave the next day to spend the rest of the summer on the lonely shores of the Grand Barachois, a shallow bay on the island of Miquelon.

"Hard to credit," remarked Cyril, "that you got a machine that records the noises those old horsehead seals makes underneath the water. Can't help but wonder what good that would be to anyone—except maybe another seal."

"We hope to determine, among other things, the distance the young Grey seal ventures from its parents as it grows in size and strength," explained Dr. Horwood earnestly.

"And what if they don't say anything? What if they figure you're getting too nosy and they don't make a sound?"

"Well, then," chuckled Dr. Horwood, "we'll have to

look for some other means of communication. Whatever we discover, it's never wasted time. There's so much
still to learn about the life of the Grey seal."

"A table!" called Cécile from the dining-room. That
evening the table had been set for a celebration. There
was a lace table-cloth; two tall, white candles on either
side of a vase full of wildflowers; and coloured paper
streamers hanging from the light fixture in the ceiling.
Andrea was surprised that Uncle Cyril's release from jail
meant so much to Madame Foliot.

However, she was not nearly as surprised as Dr. Tom
Horwood was when, with a flourish, Cécile Foliot
handed him a colourful greeting card and a bottle of
wine with a fancy ribbon around it.

"Bonne fête!" Cécile cried. *"Bonne fête!"*

"What *is* all this?" laughed Dr. Horwood.

"Madame is wishing you a happy birthday," Andrea
told him.

"What? Oh, I'm afraid there's been a mistake. My
birthday is in November. November the ninth, in fact,"
said Dr. Horwood, feeling a little embarrassed. Where in
the world had Madame Foliot got the idea that this was
his birthday?

*"Pardonne, Madame, le professeur dit que son anniver-
saire est au mois de novembre,"* Andrea began.

"Ah, mais non, mais non," insisted Cécile, and then
she retrieved a calendar from the kitchen. *"Regarde. La
fête de St. Thomas. Aujourd'hui. Le trois juillet,"* she per-
sisted, pointing to the tiny square for July the third
which did indeed have *"St. Thomas"* printed in it.

"Today is the feast of St. Thomas," Andrea explained.

"It is?" said an astonished Dr. Horwood. "If you say so then. Where I grew up, in Digby, Nova Scotia, we didn't celebrate this sort of thing."

"Eh bien! Bonne fête!" chirped Madame Cécile, handing Tom the corkscrew with which he was to open the bottle.

Philippe, who always became shy when he had to say anything in English, nevertheless volunteered to explain. "Here in St. Pierre each person have a special, ah . . . *fête.*"

"Celebration," said Andrea.

"A celebration on the day of our saint. My special day is in May."

What a brilliant idea, Andrea thought, wondering if there ever was a St. Andrea.

Cyril turned to Tom Horwood. "Look here, me son, I don't say as I understand entirely, but if they wants to give you a fine time, I'm for it." He held out his wine glass so that it clinked against the one Tom was holding. "We can count our blessings today. We got good reason to celebrate. We'll be heading for Anderson's Arm tomorrow. I'm mighty glad of that. And I'm some grateful that cousin Cécile here has been so kind to Jeffie and Andrea and to all of us."

"Well, then, a toast to Madame Cécile Foliot," said Dr. Tom Horwood, raising his glass. "I now have an excuse for another annual party I didn't even know about before."

"I'm sorry to hear that you're leaving, Andrea," said Karen Corkum. "You've helped us so much. We were hoping you could be our liaison person here in town."

"You were?" said Andrea, happily surprised.

"Yes. You see, we need someone to arrange for supplies and messages and things. We can call on our portable radio-telephone from our camp at Miquelon. The trouble is, with our French being so limited, well, we would have problems trying to communicate," explained Karen.

"Gee, I'd really like to do that for you," sighed Andrea, "only I guess I can't."

"And of course we would pay you a small salary— but if you're leaving, then I suppose we'll have to find someone else," she said, sounding disappointed.

The party went on for a long time, and at the end of it there was even a birthday cake for Tom. Everyone had a lot of fun on this unexpected and joyful occasion. But Andrea began to feel wistful. She had been offered a summer job and, what was more, it sounded like an interesting job in a place she was reluctant to leave. It was late when she finally got to bed, and she had trouble going to sleep. She wanted that job and she wanted to stay here. Could she make it happen?

CHAPTER EIGHT

NEXT MORNING FOG WAS SHROUDING ST. Pierre more thickly than ever, and it was accompanied by a cold drizzle of rain. When Andrea awoke and heard the fog-horn, she felt very gloomy. It wasn't merely the weather. She knew she should be happy because her uncle was out of jail and they were all free to leave. The problem was that she liked being here. Now it occurred to her that Cécile Foliot might let her remain at Auberge Cécile if she helped with the work, but would Aunt Pearl and Uncle Cyril permit such a thing? She *had* to find some way to stay.

The weather forced everyone to change their plans that day. Having got lost once, Cyril decided it would be wise to wait for better visibility before setting sail for Newfoundland. Dr. Horwood and Dr. Corkum also decided to postpone their journey as they preferred to begin their expedition on a day that was not quite so damp. Philippe's work day was cancelled because they were now painting the exterior doors and window sills, and it was too wet to paint outdoors. With their plans on hold, the visitors lingered over breakfast—all except Andrea. With her new plans in mind, she decided this was the time to be super-helpful. She volunteered to run down to the bakery for another loaf of bread when it appeared that more was needed. Then she washed and dried the breakfast dishes and put them away in the cupboard. When she saw Cécile dropping laundry into the washing machine, Andrea offered to keep an eye on it and, when it was done, to load it into the dryer and then to fold it up. This left Cécile free to go to the *épicier* and buy her groceries.

"Ah, ma p'tite Andrée," sighed Cécile as she was buttoning her raincoat, *"C'est dommage que tu doives partir. Tu me manqueras."*

"Et moi aussi, Madame."

"Tu aimes St. Pierre, n'est-ce pas?"

"Oui, beaucoup."

"Vraiment, tu es arrivée juste à temps," she smiled.

Andrea smiled back. It was encouraging that Cécile felt she had arrived "in the nick of time." It could mean Cécile needed her. Maybe she wanted Andrea to stay.

After the noon meal, Andrea realized this was her chance. She had to take the plunge and ask her aunt and uncle if they would let her stay on in St. Pierre.

"Well, I don't know what your mother would say, I'm sure," said Aunt Pearl, looking concerned. "Cyril and me's supposed to be looking out for you."

"I know, but Cécile is your cousin, so it's still in the family. Anyway, I can look after myself. And I have a chance to earn some money working for Dr. Horwood and Dr. Corkum, and that will help once school starts and I have to buy books and things."

"I know. I know that, my dear, but you're awful young to be away in this foreign place by your own self," argued Aunt Pearl.

Uncle Cyril had been very quiet and he looked thoughtful. He finally broke in. "I do believe Cécile is a good person and very kind. 'Tis a shame we can't have a proper talk with her about all this."

"I've already talked to her," pleaded Andrea, stretching things a little. "I know she likes me and that I'm welcome here, and she does need help. She's got a lot of tourists coming from now till the end of August. There's all the laundry and the cooking and everything. Philippe can't help her much because he's gone all day at work."

"Surely she's going to need that room you're in to rent out and make some money," Aunt Pearl reasoned.

"Yes, but you know what? There's a cute little bedroom on the third floor . . . in the attic. I could sleep up there," Andrea explained.

"You're some determined, maid," clucked Uncle Cyril. "I got to admire you for that."

"That's right! I really *will* be a maid!" laughed Andrea. "Cleaning and washing and cooking to pay for my room and board."

"Well, I suppose it might be all right," said Aunt Pearl cautiously. "I'm going home with Cyril and Jeff on the boat so you could use my return plane ticket when it's time to come back."

"Oh, Aunt Pearl, that's wonderful! Thanks a million," she cried, giving her aunt a big hug. "I'm going to miss you, all of you. It's just that this is an opportunity I don't want to miss. It's only for the summer. I'll be back in time to start school."

"Now, hold on, hold on. There's two things. First, we got to sit down and try and talk with Cécile when she gets back from the shops, and second, you got to write a letter to your mother right away," insisted Uncle Cyril.

"I will. I will," agreed Andrea.

When Cécile returned, she said she would be very pleased to have Andrea stay with her for the rest of the summer. She had been thinking of hiring someone anyway. Andrea would be ideal.

Dear Mom,

You'll never guess where I am. I'm in St. Pierre and Miquelon. It's just near Newfoundland (maybe you know that) but it's really part of France. Is it ever neat! We met this family named Foliot. They're Aunt Pearl's cousins from years ago. Madame Cécile Foliot is really nice and she asked me to stay here for the rest of the summer and help with the work. She takes in tourists. And I've also got this other summer job part time working for some scientists who are doing research here.

Cécile has a son named Philippe and he's very . . .

Andrea had just begun a new page but now she ripped it up and threw it in the waste-paper basket. It might be better not to mention Philippe. Her mom might get the wrong idea. She began the second page again:

The research has to do with seals. It's a man and a woman (they're married). They pay me to help them because they're going off on another island near here and I can look after things for them here in town.

Andrea paused and thought about what to say next. Better not say anything about Uncle Cyril getting arrested. That would make her mother worry. She continued the letter.

> It's cold here even though it's July. There's a lot
> of fog. I hope it's nice and sunny where you are, Mom.
> I hope everything is okay. How is Brad?
> In case you're wondering how we got here, it was
> in Uncle Cyril's new fishing boat. It's sort of a long
> story. Aunt Pearl says she'll write and tell you.
> I miss you a whole lot, Mom. Write soon.
> > Love and kisses,
> > Andrea

Andrea took the letter to the post office, where she bought a strange-looking stamp with a picture of an old-fashioned airplane on it. Her letter had a long way to go to reach her mother in Sierra Leone.

The next day the weather changed. The fog disappeared and was replaced by a breezy, overcast day with huge puffy clouds that sailed across the sky as far as the horizon.

"Following breeze for home. Finest kind, me son," Cyril said to Jeff. Since dawn the two of them had been down at the wharf making sure everything was ship-shape aboard the *Blanche and Marilyn*. Jeff could barely contain his excitement and happiness to be finally heading for home.

Aunt Pearl had lingered at the *auberge* to pack their belongings and to fuss over Andrea.

"I don't know, my dear. I just don't know. What if I

hear from your mother and she says you got to return to our place?"

"Then I'll come right back, okay? I promise. I've got a plane ticket. Don't worry, Aunt Pearl. Mom won't object. I mean, if she can go to Africa, why would she mind if I stayed in St. Pierre for a while? I'm not that far from Anderson's Arm—not like she is."

"I suppose," sighed Pearl. "I'd best be sending along the rest of your summer clothes then. You'll surely need them if you're to be here till the end of August."

At that point, Cécile came in with an armload of clean towels. *"Ah, Perle,"* she said with sincerity, *"ne vous inquiétez pas. Andrée sera heureuse ici. Elle m'aidera. Elle sera bientôt de retour."*

Aunt Pearl smiled, even though she hadn't understood a word.

"She says don't worry about a thing," explained Andrea.

Dr. Corkum and Dr. Horwood were also up early that morning. Andrea helped them load their equipment into a truck. They and their gear were destined for the same big wharf where the *Blanche and Marilyn* was. The scientists had hired a fishing boat to ferry them to Miquelon, a voyage of several hours. So it was a morning of farewells as Andrea waited on the wharf and waved goodbye, first to her aunt and uncle and her cousin, and then, twenty minutes later, to Karen and Tom.

When she returned to Auberge Cécile, the house was very quiet. Cécile had gone to the hairdresser. Philippe was back at work painting the school. There was no one around except the orange cat, who started meowing to be let out. For a few minutes Andrea felt terribly alone. She wondered if she had made the right decision. However, there wasn't much time to think about it. Tomorrow a family of four was due to arrive from Ottawa, and it was Andrea's job to make up their beds and be sure their rooms were dusted. After that, she had to move her clothes up to the cosy little room on the third floor, her new home for the summer.

From the small window up there, she had a bird's-eye view of the entire town. On this day she could easily see the coast of Newfoundland twenty kilometres away. Down on the street below, a man and a woman walked by pushing a stroller with a little boy in it. A small brown dog trotted along in the opposite direction, carefully watched by the orange cat.

What was going to happen during the days and weeks ahead? Would it all be wonderful and exciting, or would it turn out to be boring and awful? Andrea studied the airplane ticket to St. John's before carefully tucking it into the zippered pocket of her duffle bag. She went back to the window and stared dreamily at the street below until she saw Cécile's sea-green Renault heading back up the hill. That snapped her out of her day-dreams and she hurried downstairs. It was time to set the dinner table again.

CHAPTER NINE

"SUCH INCREDIBLE LUXURY!" DECLARED Dr. Karen Corkum as she stepped out of the upstairs bathroom at Auberge Cécile, wrapped up in a huge white towel. She was patting her hair dry with another towel. "You can't imagine what a treat it is to soak in a big bathtub full of hot water after four weeks of keeping clean with only one pail of water every day, heated over the campfire."

"Sounds awful," commented Andrea. She had been changing all the bedsheets and pillowcases in preparation for a new bunch of guests who would be arriving that afternoon.

"It's not really. You'd be surprised how well we manage—how well anyone can manage—if they use their ingenuity and figure out how to live on a simpler scale. It can be quite a lot of fun."

Karen had had to return to the town of St. Pierre because she had lost a filling from one of her teeth. Andrea had arranged a dentist appointment for her. Karen's tooth had been repaired and now she had a day left over before she had to return to the campsite and her work.

"I've always loved camping," Karen chatted as she ate her breakfast, "but I must admit this is a welcome holiday for me to be here. And, oh, how I love this bread! This is the same kind you send us every week, isn't it?"

"Sure is," Andrea confirmed. "Direct from Boulangerie Rémy."

"I'm going to miss it when we leave," Karen remarked. "Goodness, summer is half over and we still have so much work to do. Odd thing, when we started our research early in July, we thought we were observing a stable population."

"What's that?"

"A fixed number of seals. An extended family whose members live together. But lately . . . well, we don't know. A couple of them have disappeared, gone away somewhere."

"There was something I was wondering, Karen," Andrea ventured.

"What's that?"

"Doesn't it get kind of lonely up there? Just you and Tom and those seals?"

"Not as much as you'd think. For one thing, we are quite busy with our work. And then, from time to time, we do see the occasional person. The other day there were a couple of back-packers, from Denmark. They stopped to chat with us. And before that there were the two men who check the navigational markers. We saw them in their boat so we invited them to join us for coffee. And, of course, some nights there are . . . those lights. They reassure us that we're not entirely alone in the world."

"Lights? What kind of lights?"

"Out on the ocean. A boat of some sort."

"Who?"

"Haven't a clue."

"Aren't you afraid?"

"No. They're way offshore somewhere. Sometimes

Tom and I amuse ourselves speculating about what they're doing."

"Maybe they're smugglers," suggested Andrea.

"We wondered about that but I doubt it somehow. They never come ashore. They don't appear to rendez-vous with anyone else. Anyway, it's not our concern."

"Spooky."

"It is, in a way."

"Oooh. I would love to see something like that. I love mysteries."

"Really?" Karen laughed. "I guess I did too when I was your age. Well, I suppose I had better get going. Seeing as I'm here in the midst of things, I might as well use my time to do a little sight-seeing and maybe some shopping. Perhaps I'll go back to that perfume shop. Wasn't it fun? Do you want to come with me, Andrea?"

"Damn it. I mean, darn. I can't. I have to get the laundry done before Cécile gets back from the store. Then I have to peel the potatoes and after that I have to set the table, and all that stuff," Andrea grumbled.

"Of course. Well, another time then," said Karen warmly.

Shortly after Karen left, Cécile returned with the groceries and she also brought the mail. At last there was a letter for Andrea from her mother.

Sierra Leone, July 20

Dearest Andrea,

I was so happy to get your letter. It's too bad it took so long to get here but I guess the mail is slow where you are and even slower where we are.

I hope you're okay, sweetheart. I was surprised to learn you are in St. Pierre instead of Anderson's Arm, but I also got a letter from Aunt Pearl who assured me you are in good hands. I never knew she had a cousin out there. Just remember to say thank you to her for being so kind. But in St. Pierre it would be *"merci,"* right?

Brad and I are truly enjoying our work here. We are training teachers who will continue this work after we leave. We are renting a nice little house and we do have electricity but only for two hours a day. That is enough because it is very warm so we don't need any heat except for cooking.

The only thing I don't like is the snakes. Most of them are poisonous. We have to be careful where we walk at night.

Along with teaching literacy skills, Brad is organizing carpentry classes for the boys and I am starting sewing for the girls.

Remember that I miss you very much. Brad sends his love to you. Write soon.

All my love,

Mom

Andrea folded the letter up and put it back inside the blue air-mail envelope, intrigued by the stamp with a bright red bird on it. She tried to picture her mother in that far-away place. She didn't like snakes either. Maybe, she day-dreamed for a fleeting moment, Brad might get bitten by one of those poisonous snakes and then her mom would have to come home, and the two of them would move back to Toronto, and it would be just like it used to be. Then she thought about the same snake biting her mother. That was horrible. She didn't want to think about that. She put the letter in the pocket of her jeans and went back out to the dining-room to clear away the breakfast dishes.

August had been the busiest month for tourists in St. Pierre. Most of the time all the rooms at Auberge Cécile were occupied. Cécile and Andrea rarely had any time to themselves. However, Cécile was such a cheerful person that working with her didn't feel like hard work. Throughout those busy weeks in the middle of summer, she and Andrea had become very good friends. Andrea wouldn't have missed this experience for the world. She enjoyed meeting the guests and often helped with the translating. Most of the guests had been a lot of fun and some of them even left a tip for her when they checked out. As well as her work at the *auberge*, Andrea loved traipsing all over town to get things done for Karen and Tom.

Everything had been perfect, except for one thing. All along she had been hoping to get to know Philippe a little better. A lot better, actually. He was friendly enough, in his way, but the trouble was that he was always so busy. He worked long hours every day and then almost every evening he was out playing soccer. When he finished playing soccer, he and his buddies usually ended up at a discothèque called *Le Joinville*. By the time he got home, it was late and Andrea had already gone to bed. She was dying to know what went on at *Le Joinville*. She had dropped a few hints to Philippe that she was interested in seeing what it was like. Unfortunately, Cécile had overheard her, and she told Andrea in no uncertain terms that no one was allowed inside until he or she was sixteen years old. It was the only time Cécile had been really stern with her. She said the police would come and throw people out of the disco if they were too young. Andrea got scared then. She didn't want any more encounters with the police. But she was still curious to know what went on inside this popular night spot.

One morning in late August, Andrea was surprised, and pleased, to see that Philippe was still at home, dawdling over a second cup of coffee at the breakfast table.

"Aren't you going to work this morning?" Andrea asked him. He was usually out of the house before eight o'clock.

"Ni aujourd'hui, ni demain," replied Philippe.

"Pourquoi?"

"Mon travail est fini. Toutes les écoles sont peintes maintenant," he shrugged.

So he was out of a job, Andrea thought, realizing that he would probably be staying around the house now and she might see him more often. Her work was dwindling as well. They were expecting a couple of tourists from the United States this week but no one else after that. As Cécile had remarked at breakfast, once the nights grew chilly and the northerly winds strengthened, the tourist season was almost finished for another year.

That morning Philippe was engrossed in a French motorcycle magazine called *Moto Verte*. He told Andrea that he hoped his summer earnings would be enough to buy a Peugeot 103. She peered over his shoulder at a photograph of the trim red motorbike. Yes, she thought to herself, it would be neat if he got one. She could even picture herself riding on it, too.

The phone rang.

"Damn it. Darn it," muttered Andrea under her breath. She didn't want anything to interrupt the delightful day-dream she was spinning of zooming around town on a motorbike with Philippe, the two of them, close together.

The phone kept ringing. Andrea picked it up.

"Allô."

"Hello, Andrea. Over," called Karen Corkum. Her voice sounded faint and static-ridden over the radio connection from their camp on Miquelon island. She and Tom had now spent nearly eight weeks studying the habits of the Grey seal.

"Hi, Karen, what can I get for you? Over." Andrea reached for a pencil and notepad.

"We won't be here much longer so we don't need a lot this week. Could you get us some more of that wonderful bread — four loaves — and a few of those delicious French pastries? And a couple more tins of that pâté we like. And some Brie cheese and a dozen eggs. And do you think you could locate an underwater camera filter, one that fits a Zeiss 400? You might have to try a few places but we really need it. Over."

"Mmm-hmm. Okay," replied Andrea, jotting things down.

"And Andrea, Tom and I were wondering if you would like to come up here for a few days? Do you think Cécile could spare you? Is the inn busy now? Over."

"No, we're not busy here at all. Over."

"Great. When you get all the stuff together for the boat tomorrow, pack up your sleeping bag and come on out, too. This is actually a very interesting place and I have the feeling you'll like it. We'll be closing out our camp on Monday or Tuesday so you can return to St. Pierre with us then. How does that sound? Over."

"Fantastic! I'll be there," cried Andrea. "Over and out!"

"Guess what," she said excitedly, after hanging up the phone. "Karen and Tom have invited me to go up there for a visit — to Grand Barachois. Gosh, I wonder what it's like?"

"Grand Barachois? A lot of . . . ah, sand," replied Philippe, who had to pause and think of the correct words.

"Sand? Is that all?" she asked, disappointed.

"It is possible to see many . . . *loups marins*," he added.

"Of course, the Grey seals. That's why they're there."

"It is possible also to see the bones of whales. And sometimes you will see . . . *un navire naufragé*," added Philippe.

"A what?"

"*Un navire naufragé.* I don't know the English."

"Neither do I but I'll get your dictionary. It's in my room." Andrea darted upstairs and ran back down with his French-English school dictionary, which she had borrowed for the summer.

"*Navire naufragé* means a shipwreck. Wow! That would be awesome!"

"*Anciens* shipwrecks. A long time ago. Me, I like that place very much. My father—before he is died—we go often in his boat but now . . . I did not see it for a long time," he concluded a bit sadly.

"Gee, that's too bad. But, hey, you know what? Maybe you should come too, seeing as you're not working right now. Karen and Tom wouldn't mind, I'll bet. You could probably help them out. They're taking down their camp next week," explained Andrea, hopeful that this would be a rare opportunity to get better acquainted with Philippe.

Philippe's eyes brightened and he put down his magazine. "I think that is a happy voyage for me," he smiled.

"*Will be* a happy voyage," Andrea corrected him. "*C'est au temps futur.*"

"Yes, the future," he grinned. "The happy future."

CHAPTER TEN

LE PETIT CHEVALIER PUT-PUTTED SLOWLY away from the wharf. At the helm of the big dory sat Théophile Detcheverry, a hefty man with a large nose and a tiny grey beard that barely covered his chin. He had been a fisherman for most of his sixty-seven years but this summer had the less arduous job of ferrying weekly supplies to the two Canadian scientists camped on the shore of the Grand Barachois.

Andrea was beginning to feel quite at home in boats now, even though *Le Petit Chevalier* wasn't nearly as big as Uncle Cyril's scallop dragger. She crouched down in the bow of the open boat and zipped up her leather jacket. The breeze was chilly despite the sunshine.

The sunbeams on the waves created a dazzling pattern. Andrea gazed into the sombre green depths, hypnotized by the darting arrows of light which, in a peculiar way, reminded her of the twinkling lights in the big stores and office buildings in downtown Toronto at Christmas.

Toronto seemed so far away now. Andrea thought about the way things had been before her mother married Brad and before Brad got the crazy idea to go teaching school in Africa. She thought about her best friend from Willow Drive School and wondered what Suzy would be doing right then. Andrea had promised to write to Suzy, and here it was the end of August and she still hadn't found time to do it. She vowed she would do so as soon as she got back to Auberge Cécile. She had so many things to tell her.

Philippe was sitting in the stern of the boat alongside skipper Théophile. He was wearing a baggy, cable-knit sweater his mother had knitted. Navy blue suited him. He hadn't had a haircut all summer and his curly hair was getting rather long. He really was very cute, Andrea decided.

Occasionally he and the older man chatted quietly in French but most of the time Philippe seemed lost in his own thoughts as the old engine propelled the boat resolutely towards the mouth of the harbour. As they were passing a wharf in front of a windowless, concrete building, Théophile pointed towards it and began talking rapidly about a matter that obviously disturbed him.

"Regarde ce bâtiment, mademoiselle!" he shouted to Andrea over the thudding of the engine. *"Le frigorifique. Tout abandonné maintenant. C'est terrible, n'est-ce pas?"*

Andrea noticed the large, featureless building. It was a fish-freezing plant and had once been the busiest place in St. Pierre. Not now.

"Pas de morue," lamented Théophile, shaking his head sadly.

No more codfish. Andrea was beginning to understand the situation. A hundred men and women had once made their living cutting and packing tons of fish every day and now they were unemployed. Too many people had been taking too much fish from the entire Atlantic Ocean. It was no wonder the *St. Pierrais* were so possessive of the small ocean territory around their islands where they had mistakenly arrested Uncle Cyril.

The dory chugged past the flat island of Ile aux Marins and then the high island called Grand Colombier, a place where puffins built their nests. After that they were in open water, heading for the big islands of Langlade and Miquelon. Few people lived on Langlade, just summer cottagers and campers. Most of Miquelon was uninhabited, too, except for a small village at the north end. Ninety per cent of the people of St. Pierre and Miquelon lived in the town of St. Pierre.

Langlade and Miquelon were connected by a long isthmus known as La Dune. True to Philippe's description, there certainly was a lot of sand. Along both sides of the isthmus white, sandy beaches stretched on and on and on. *Le Petit Chevalier* travelled parallel to them for half an hour before finally reaching a narrow opening in the dunes leading into a vast, salt-water lagoon called Le Grand Barachois. This was where Tom and Karen had set up their camp.

The dory moved very slowly now as Théophile carefully steered it into the lagoon through a maze of channels and sand-bars. As they approached the far shore, they could see three small tents and Tom Horwood and Karen Corkum waving to them.

"Welcome to Grand Barachois!" called Tom.

Tom and Karen both had suntans. Tom had grown a beard. Karen looked relaxed and prettier now. Her long, dark brown hair was gathered at the nape of her neck with a blue plastic hair clip. Andrea remembered purchasing it and sending it up with the supplies several weeks earlier.

Théophile inched the bow of his boat into the sandy shore. Andrea and Philippe removed their shoes and waded ashore, making several trips to unload the cartons of food and other supplies.

Andrea felt sure Karen and Tom would be really pleased she had been able to find the right camera filter for them. She figured it might be a good idea to show it to them before she mentioned inviting Philippe to stay too.

"Terrific! You found one," exclaimed Karen, with a big smile.

"I had to go to four different shops but I finally got one, the last filter they had, too," Andrea explained smugly.

"Sure, that's okay," said Tom casually, when she cautiously told them about Philippe, "but he'll have to sleep in the tent with the camera equipment. The bed-and-breakfast accommodation around here isn't as good as it is in St. Pierre," he chuckled.

Indeed it wasn't. There were no buildings or any other signs of human life as far as the eye could see— just sand and tussock grass and surf and sky and birds.

The tide was falling so Théophile did not linger. He departed, and as soon as the sound of the boat's engine faded into the distance, a seal appeared in the channel close to the camp.

"Look!" shrieked Andrea, startled by the sudden appearance of the sleek black head that had emerged from the shallow water only a stone's throw from where she stood.

"Yep, there's old Sammy," said Tom.

"Sammy?" asked Andrea.

"We gave them names," explained Karen. "Just wait a moment and the next one you'll see will probably be Slippery. She's Sammy's wife—one of his wives. He always pops up first, then she follows."

Andrea sat down on the sand, fascinated. Sure enough, in a few minutes another gleaming, dark grey head appeared a dozen feet from Sammy. The two mammals stared at the four people on the shore for several moments, apparently as fascinated by the sight of human beings as Andrea was by the seals.

Karen handed Andrea her binoculars. She watched for a long time, then suddenly, as though a signal had been given, the seals disappeared below the surface of the water.

"They look like dogs—great big dogs without ears. And all those whiskers!" observed Andrea.

"They're a lot bigger than dogs," said Tom. "Sammy weighs at least three hundred pounds, Slippery somewhat less."

"Look, there's Sally," called Karen, pointing to yet another seal's head that had popped up in the water.

"Sally may be Sammy's other wife. Or she could be their daughter from last year. We're not certain."

Andrea watched Sally through the binoculars until the seal slid silently beneath the surface to some secret destination of her own.

"You know what I think?" said Andrea firmly. "I think it's really gross the way people club baby seals to death out on the ice in the winter. I saw it on TV one time."

"Those weren't Grey seals, though," explained Tom. "Grey seals don't whelp on the ice as a rule. What you saw on television were Harp seals. For the most part, Grey seals give birth to their young on offshore islands. They aren't slaughtered for their pelts the way the Harp seals are."

"I'm glad to hear that," said Andrea fervently.

"Mind you, the Grey seals have their enemies, too. Fishermen don't like them."

"Why not?"

"They see them as competition—for the fish. Fish stocks have been dwindling for quite a long time now. Some people prefer to blame the seals instead of mankind's greed."

"And speaking of fish, I think it's time we started making supper," interrupted Karen. "You must be starving. We'll be seeing lots more seals. Scruffy and Sebastian and Stanley haven't arrived yet but I expect they'll

be along soon. They're a bunch of young bachelors. They like to go out roaming on a Saturday night."

"Like me," laughed Philippe.

Andrea laughed, too. However, this was one Saturday night he wouldn't be out clowning around with his soccer buddies. He had no choice but to stay right there in camp.

"Got a job for you two," added Karen. "How about gathering firewood—some driftwood from along the beach? Our propane supply is getting low so we have to cook over a camp-fire tonight. Hope you both like clam chowder!"

Andrea and Philippe wandered barefoot in the white sand, picking up weathered sticks and boards.

"*Qu'est-ce que c'est là-bas?*" asked Andrea, pointing to something moving in the far distance.

"*Ah! Chevaux sauvages,*" answered Philippe.

"*Wild* horses?"

"*Oui. Ils habitent La Dune.*"

"*Ils n'appartiennent à personne?*"

"*Personne.*"

"That's awesome," said Andrea, thrilled by the discovery that horses wandered around freely here and didn't belong to anyone but themselves. She watched the three grazing horses for several minutes until they eventually cantered off beyond the sandy horizon. Once again the landscape was still.

"*Cherchons un navire naufragé,*" said Andrea.

"Okay," agreed Philippe. "*Quand j'étais petit il y a eu un grand naufrage près d'ici.*"

They searched in every direction but there was no sign of a shipwreck from long ago. Where was it now? *"L'épave, où est-elle maintenant?"* she asked.

"Disparue. Au cours des grandes tempêtes d'hiver, le sable se déplace. La dune change de forme chaque année."

"Ooooh, wicked," Andrea exhaled with a small shiver, trying to imagine what this windswept place would look like during a ferocious winter storm when the sands shifted and mysterious things were unearthed while others disappeared.

They hiked back to the camp, clutching bundles of driftwood. Tom and Karen were organizing supper. Karen was tending the fire under a big kettle of chowder made from clams Tom had dug up on the beach that morning when the tide was out. Near the fire was a long, low table he had constructed from weathered boards he had found washed up on the shore earlier in the summer. Now he was busy setting out plastic dishes containing butter, cheese, pâté, canned sardines, hard-boiled eggs, and fresh French bread.

When everything was ready, the four of them sat cross-legged in the sand around the table. They ate and talked and laughed for a long time as the fire burned down, the sun set, and the western sky gradually changed from blue to the colour of apricots and peaches.

Philippe seemed more relaxed this evening than Andrea had ever seen him—and so were Karen and Tom, who seemed truly glad to have the young people there with them. As she stole a glance at Philippe's shadowed profile, it occurred to Andrea that this was the most romantic evening of her entire life. She wished it could last for ever.

"So, Phil, what do you think you'll do when you finish school?" Tom enquired.

"I think about the military, perhaps," replied Philippe. "There is not much work here now."

"The French military?" asked Tom.

"Of course. It is a possibility for *St. Pierrais*. But . . . I don't know. France is . . . *très* . . ."

"Very far," coached Andrea quietly.

"Yes, very far. Perhaps I do not be happy if I go."

Andrea decided not to correct his grammar this time. He was trying hard to express himself and doing very well, and she didn't want to discourage him. She glanced at him again in the glow from the embers of the camp-fire. She could picture him in a soldier's uniform, maybe one like the St. Pierre *gendarmes* wore. There might be medals on his chest, medals for bravery. And some kind of a smart cap—and then she suddenly realized he would be a zillion miles away in France. How would she ever have a chance to see him dressed in his uniform? Would he be coming back to St. Pierre? Would she?

"True," nodded Karen Corkum. "France is rather a long way. And it has a different lifestyle from here."

"My brother—he live in France," said Philippe. "He is a soldier. I have another brother—in Montreal."

Montreal. That sounded better to Andrea. Closer to home. She could visualize a trip to Montreal much more easily than a trip to France.

"I have one more brother. In Newfoundland," continued Philippe.

Better still, Andrea thought and then ventured to ask, *"As-tu faites un séjour chez ton frère en Terre-Neuve?"*

"Pas encore. Mais à Noël nous irons à St. Jean, ma mère et moi. Mon frère a épousé une jeune fille de Terre-Neuve. Ils attendent un bébé bientôt."

So Philippe and Cécile would be spending Christmas in St. John's, Newfoundland—which wasn't an impossible distance from Anderson's Arm.

Tom Horwood yawned. "Well, you young people may have all kinds of energy to stay up talking all night but I think we should turn in. Around here we go to bed with the sun and get up with the sun. No electric lights to distract us."

After they had cleaned up the camp-site and washed the dishes, Andrea crawled into the little pup tent that had been set up for her. She snuggled into her sleeping bag and squirmed around, making dents in the sand so she would be more comfortable. As she lay there, she wondered if this was something like the place where her mother was working in Africa. No, it would be hot there. Here it was cool and there weren't any trees. There weren't any snakes either, thank goodness.

She and Philippe were going to search for the remains of an old shipwreck in the morning. Even if they didn't find one, they could just sit and look at the seals for hours. Maybe she ought to think about studying marine biology. Maybe . . . lots of things. Then she drifted off to sleep.

CHAPTER ELEVEN

ANDREA OPENED HER EYES AND STARED groggily up at the green nylon above her head. Had she been dreaming? She was sure she had heard a loud, sharp bang, like a fire-cracker close at hand. She propped herself up on one elbow and listened intently for a moment. Then she wiggled out of her sleeping bag and crawled over to the door flap to look out. The eastern sky was streaked with the first light of dawn, the ocean was a sombre grey, and the surrounding landscape uniformly beige. It was incredibly quiet. There was a cool breeze and she began to shiver. She reached for her leather jacket and put it on over her pink pyjamas.

There was no sign of life from Tom and Karen's tent, nor from the small red one where Philippe slept alongside the camera equipment. It must have been a dream. Maybe, she yawned, she should just go back to bed.

Then she heard it again—this time a series of gunshots. What was going on? Suddenly Philippe bolted from the red tent, yanking on his blue jeans and sweater.

"*Qu'est-ce qui arrive?*" he blurted, catching sight of Andrea peering out of her tent.

"*Je ne sais pas,*" Andrea replied, trembling more from fright than from the cold.

"*C'était un coup de fusil?*"

"*Je pense que oui.*"

Now Tom emerged from the other tent, followed by a sleepy-looking Karen. They were both wearing striped pyjamas.

"What in hell? Is someone starting a war?" Tom spluttered.

Karen darted back into the tent to get a pair of binoculars. Then she scanned the cool, grey horizon. "Over there!" she pointed.

Near the entrance to Grand Barachois was a small boat with two people standing up in it. They were pointing guns at an unseen target.

"What the devil do they think they're doing?" asked Tom angrily. "This isn't hunting season."

"Look out there!" Andrea cried. "There's a bigger boat further out at sea."

They stared where Andrea was pointing. A vessel that looked like a long-liner appeared to be anchored about half a kilometre from the shore.

Bang! Bang! Bang! Bang!

"For the love of—*Get down! Get down!*" ordered Tom. "Those shots were in our direction!"

The four of them dropped to the sand.

"Ohmigosh! Is somebody trying to kill us?" whispered Andrea.

"No. I doubt they were aiming at us. Probably never imagined anyone was here but whatever they're shooting at is in this direction. What the dickens are they up to?" grumbled Tom angrily.

"We must go to the big dune . . . over there," said Philippe urgently. "There it is possible to see—"

"Good thinking, Phil. You two stay here. We'll check it out," Tom ordered.

Crouching low, Tom and Philippe sprinted the hundred yards to the dune and slipped behind it. After a minute or two, Tom waved to Karen and Andrea to join them. Soon they were all lying panting side by side on their stomachs just below the grassy crest of a sand dune where they had a clear view of the entire barachois.

Tom handed Philippe the binoculars. "Would you take a look and tell us if those guys are people you know? And that long-liner out there—whose boat is that?"

Philippe scanned the surface of the ocean.

"Maybe they're spies," Andrea suggested in a low voice.

"Ha!" chuckled Philippe. "What is it they spy here in this place?"

"I don't know. Maybe there's a secret rocket-launching site. Or there could be a neutron bomb testing range around here somewhere."

Philippe handed the binoculars back to Tom. *"Ah, Andrée,"* he grinned. *"Quelle imagination vive!* I think you see too much television, eh?" He reached over and tousled her hair which, Andrea realized, she hadn't even combed yet this morning.

"Is it anyone you recognize?" enquired Tom.

"Non," replied Philippe. "She is not from St. Pierre, this boat."

"Maybe a fishing vessel from Miquelon?" suggested Karen.

"Non," said Philippe. "There is no . . . *grand bateau de pêche* . . . like that in Miquelon."

Bang! Bang! Bang!

They ducked their heads and lay in fearful silence for a moment.

"They do not catch fish, this boat," observed

Philippe as he peered over the crest of the dune. "There is no . . . *mouette* . . ."

"*Mouette?* What's that?" asked Andrea.

"It is birds who follow a fishing boat. Look . . . that bird there . . ." he pointed to one on the shore.

"Oh, a gull. A seagull," Andrea translated.

"Son of a gun! You're right!" cried Tom, noticing the absence of birds around the vessel. He knew that seagulls always follow a working fishing boat, waiting for scraps to be thrown overboard. "So just what are they up to?"

"Drug smugglers," Andrea speculated.

"I don't think so," said Tom. "Otherwise there would be someone on shore to collect the stuff. There's not a soul around here, except us, of course. And what's more, smugglers wouldn't be firing off guns and making their presence known."

Bang! Bang!

"They weren't in our direction this time," observed Tom. "Whatever they're after is moving around."

The sun had risen and visibility was improving. By now the colour of the ocean was closer to blue than it was to grey. Andrea took her turn with the binoculars, aiming them alternately at the row-boat and then out to sea where the larger boat was anchored. Gradually the stern of the vessel faced the shore, and Andrea could see there was a name and a home port painted on it.

"I can almost read her name!" squealed Andrea, squinting into the binoculars. "Something with a lot of letters close together. Underneath it says . . . mmm . . . Port McLean or maybe Port McLeod . . . Port McSomething, N.S. Or is it N.B.? One or the other."

"Nova Scotia or New Brunswick. So they're Canadians, for heaven's sake," said Karen disapprovingly.

"Why on earth are they here?" Tom asked again.

Bang!

Seconds after the rifle shot, Andrea watched as one of the men jumped out of the boat and waded through the shallow water alongside a sand-bar. At the end of it lay his quarry—a Grey seal, writhing in its death agony.

"Oh, no!" moaned Andrea, lowering the binoculars. "He's shot that seal!"

"Damn!" cried Karen.

"Damned idiots!" added Tom. "I should have guessed! They're bloody bounty hunters."

"He killed that seal!" Andrea wailed, tears streaming down her face.

"Now, now, Andrea, don't cry," said Karen, trying to comfort her with a hug, her own eyes wet with tears.

" 'Bounty hunters'?" What is that?" asked Philippe.

"Until recently in Canada there was a bounty—money, that is—paid by our government for every Grey seal that was killed. It was a measure that was supposed to protect fish stocks, the assumption being that the seals eat too much fish. It's still a contentious issue. And, as it turned out, fish stocks have declined anyway, regardless of how many seals there are."

"These men will take dead seals to Canada for money?" enquired Philippe.

"The bounty has been removed—only these yahoos

don't seem to know that. The way it worked, they had to present the dead seal's jaw-bone to a Fisheries officer. Then they could collect fifty dollars. Of course there are people, regrettably, who are so bloodthirsty they want to kill seals anyway," Tom explained.

"Jaw-bone? *Qu'est-ce que c'est?*" Philippe asked Andrea.

"*La mâchoire,*" Andrea translated. "You mean they're going to . . . remove the jaw-bone?" She looked at Tom, horrified.

"Yup. Take a look," said Tom, clenching his teeth and offering her the binoculars. "They're doing it now."

"Oh, no! No! I won't look! I can't!" moaned Andrea, as more tears ran down her cheeks. "Which one is it? Is it Sammy, or Slippery or Sebastian?"

"There's no way of knowing right now," replied Karen sadly. "We'll find out later when that one doesn't show up."

"They might kill the others, too. Can't we stop them?" pleaded Andrea.

"I think not. Those men are armed, and damn careless, too! Idiots! They could easily kill one of us by accident," Tom growled.

"But this is not . . . *légitime,*" exclaimed Philippe. "They come to Miquelon and kill our seals. Those seals belong to us."

"Absolutely," agreed Karen.

"They must be stopped!" Philippe insisted.

"How? All we've got is a canoe," argued Tom.

"The French navy has a . . . *frégate*. It would not be a problem for them," noted Philippe.

"The French navy is a long way from here," said Tom.

"Pas du tout!" Philippe protested. "In St. Pierre right now there is a naval exercise. This *frégate* . . . she arrived yesterday."

"No kidding?"

"Yes, I saw it, too," added Andrea, "when we were on our way up here in Théophile's boat."

"Do you suppose," asked Tom, "that they would help? We might be able to reach them on the radio-phone."

"Why not?" Karen asked.

"Tell you what," said Tom. "Karen and I will stay here and keep an eye on these jerks. You two . . . go back to our tent where the radio-phone is and try to raise the authorities down in St. Pierre. I know it's awfully early and it's Sunday morning, but see if you can get hold of somebody. Try and persuade them to get the Fisheries patrol or somebody to come up here right away."

Hardly bothering to duck their heads, Andrea and Philippe raced across the expanse of sand between the look-out and Tom and Karen's tent. As they reached it, Andrea realized she was still wearing her pink pyjamas with her black leather jacket over them. Her clothes and hair were sprinkled with sand. What must Philippe think of her, looking like this? Of course, he was covered with sand, too. Well, there were other things to think about right now. How were they going to persuade the French navy to come to the rescue of a family of Grey seals?

CHAPTER TWELVE

"ALLÔ! ALLÔ! ST. PIERRE RADIO!" CALLED Philippe impatiently, pressing the transmission switch on the microphone of the portable radio-telephone.

No reply.

"Oh, God, what if it's broken?" groaned Andrea, looking alarmed.

"Un moment . . . j'écoute . . . allô."

"St. Pierre ici," said a distant voice.

"C'est VOBW portatif. La Gendarmerie, s'il vous plaît."

The telephone connection was made immediately. Philippe was soon talking to a policeman at the other end of the line. At times Andrea could barely understand him as the volley of words bounced back and forth. *"Oui. Deux Canadiens. Oui, deux fusils. Nous les avons vus. Oui. Okay. Oui."*

"What did he say? What did he say?" Andrea was dying to know.

"It is . . . um . . . *illégal* . . ."

"Against the law."

"For Canadians to hunt in St. Pierre. He will ask the navy to help."

"Terrific!"

"But he does not know if they will do this. It is not the responsibility of the navy. Perhaps, because the Fisheries patrol boat is, ah, rather slow to come here, then the navy may come."

"Come on, let's get back and tell Karen and Tom. Hurry."

As they left the tent, they heard a distant shot. They immediately dropped to the ground and began to crawl on their hands and knees. They hadn't gone far when Tom called out to them.

"It's okay. You can get up. The two guys are rowing out to the other boat."

"You mean they're escaping?" gasped Andrea.

"Did you get hold of anyone on the phone?"

"Yes, yes! Philippe asked the police to ask the navy and we think they might be coming," said Andrea triumphantly.

"But not certain," Philippe cautioned.

Tom shrugged. "Well, not much chance anyone could catch them before they leave St. Pierre territorial waters but at least they are on their way and good riddance to them. Let's get a fire built and make some breakfast. I don't know about the rest of you but I'm starving."

They all were. Andrea and Philippe quickly gathered more driftwood. Karen began assembling a frying pan, dishes, knives, and forks. Twenty minutes later, as they stood around waiting for the water to boil for coffee, Philippe suddenly called for silence.

"Ecoutez! Qu'est-ce que c'est que ça?"

Somewhere in the distance was a muffled thud-thud-thud-thud-thud-thud, accompanied by a high-pitched whine. The sound grew louder. Karen was the first to spot the source as she scanned the sky with her

binoculars. A helicopter was skimming over the hills of Langlade and heading in their direction.

The two Canadian hunters were now back on board their long-liner and were hauling their skiff up on the deck. Andrea stood on the shore and watched them closely through the binoculars, still hoping she could make out the name of the ship in case that information would be useful to the police. However, within minutes, the small camouflage-coloured helicopter flew directly towards the vessel and hovered directly above.

"Hurray!" yelled Andrea. "They're going to arrest them!"

"Hold on," cautioned Tom. "Those guys aren't big international crooks, as far as we know. All they're guilty of is hunting illegally. It's one thing for the crew of the chopper to spot them and identify them and quite another matter to have them arrested. The important thing is to scare them off and make sure they don't come back."

"But they killed one of the seals you were studying!" Andrea protested indignantly.

"I know. And that's a real shame but it hardly warrants a chase on the high seas," Karen reasoned.

"Well, I think it does," Andrea insisted angrily. "Why should they get away with it? Why should any of those seals be killed at all?"

"Whoa, there," said Tom, trying to calm her. "Grey seals are not on the endangered list, you know. They're not about to become extinct. Even scientists have to kill them sometimes in order to study them properly. We don't like doing it, of course."

Andrea was in no mood to be reasonable. "I should hope you wouldn't like it! And as for killing them just for some bounty money, I think that's disgusting. Don't you want to punish them? That seal was like a friend of yours!"

She turned away from them and ran down to the edge of the shore where, her arms crossed tightly in front of her, she glared angrily out over the water as the helicopter flew in slow, menacing circles above the long-liner. "I hate you, you seal killers! I hate you!" she screamed, even though no one could hear her over the noise of the helicopter.

Philippe walked down to the shore and stood beside her, putting his hand on her shoulder. "Hey, Andrée, don't be angry like that," he said softly.

"I can't help it," she said firmly. "I hate people who kill!"

"Sure, but—come on with us. There is coffee ready."

"I hate coffee, too!" she snarled, with a sour face. Then Philippe winked at her. She couldn't help but smile back at him.

"Look at it this way," reasoned Tom, who was starting to fry some bacon in the iron frying pan, "those guys on board are undoubtedly scared witless right about now."

"I certainly hope so," agreed Andrea with a wicked grin. "I wouldn't mind if they were scared to death."

The helicopter swung away from the ship and headed towards the shore. Soon it was flying in a circle above their camp. The four of them waved excitedly at the pilot who landed not far from where they stood. The huge propeller blew sand in every direction before it gradually ground to a halt. Two young men in flight uniforms jumped out and ran towards them.

"Merci! Merci beaucoup!" shouted Tom Horwood.

His French really isn't very good, thought Andrea. He pronounced *"merci"* as if it was "mercy." At least he *is* trying though, she allowed.

The helicopter belonged to the French navy frigate that was moored in the harbour of St. Pierre. The crew had been preparing for a routine exercise that morning when the St. Pierre police asked their commander to investigate a foreign vessel off the coast of Miquelon. The pilot and the navigator had been challenged by the assignment and had carried it out with *élan.*

"We told those *matelots* that if they ever came back into these territorial waters, they would be arrested," said the navigator in excellent English.

"Oui, la Bastille!" the pilot admonished with mock authority, making everyone laugh at the prospect of sending two hunters off to the most formidable prison in France for having killed a seal.

"We gave them a shower to remember. Our downdraft blew sea water all over them. They will not return," proclaimed the young navigator.

Philippe was absolutely fascinated by the helicopter, and the pilot invited him to sit inside while he explained how it worked. Tom joined them and together they inspected all the dials, levers, lights, arrows, and buttons.

"Just look at us, Andrea," laughed Karen. "We're still in our pyjamas, except Philippe. Those airmen must think we've been having a pyjama party on the beach this morning! They'll never believe we're scientists who are serious about our work."

"I'm going into my tent to get dressed," said Andrea, suddenly self-conscious.

"Me too," added Karen, "and then we'll see about that breakfast. I'm famished. And you know what?"

"What?"

"It's Sunday. This is the day we have pancakes for breakfast—with maple syrup. And seeing as this is our final Sunday here, we have to finish off all the maple syrup today. No use carrying it back to Nova Scotia."

"Is there enough for them?" asked Andrea, tilting her head towards the two airmen.

"Sure. Go ahead and invite them. How often do they get asked to a breakfast party in a place like La Dune?"

"Okay, I will," said Andrea happily.

It was a breakfast none of them would forget. The pilot and the navigator were only a few years older than Philippe. It was their first visit to St. Pierre and Miquelon and they were curious about everything. They had never seen seals before and were fascinated when two of them appeared in the barachois close by. They were very interested in the scientific study that Karen and Tom were making. But what delighted them most was the maple syrup. They had never tasted it before. In France it was an expensive luxury. By the time they had finished their pancakes, there wasn't a drop left.

"Sirop d'érable," said the young pilot as he swished the last bit of pancake around on the Melmac plate. *"C'est merveilleux!"*

The helicopter crew didn't stay long as they had to report back to their ship. They thanked their hosts for *"un bon souvenir de Miquelon."* Within one minute the gigantic blade began to whirl, again blowing sand all over their camp. The helicopter lifted noisily from the ground and soon disappeared into the southern sky.

"Well," declared Tom Horwood. "Unless we get any other unexpected company this morning, we might just possibly find time to start packing up our camp."

CHAPTER THIRTEEN

PHILIPPE WAS ENGROSSED IN HIS MOTOR-cycle magazine again when Andrea came downstairs for breakfast. It was a different magazine this time but he evidently found it just as interesting as the last one. This was Andrea's final day at Auberge Cécile, at least for the summer. Already she was talking about return-ing next year—if Cécile asked her, if Aunt Pearl and Uncle Cyril didn't object, if her mom and Brad didn't have any more wacko ideas like all of them moving to Africa.

Tom Horwood and Karen Corkum had left the day before. They were pleased to have gathered so much information and hoped to come back next year, too, although that would depend on getting a government grant to pay for a second expedition.

It seemed possible that, by the following summer, Philippe might own a motorbike. Andrea could picture the two of them zipping around St. Pierre, stopping now and then at some little café for a cold drink. This was such a far-out place.

Andrea figured her mom would like it here. Maybe next summer, her mom could come, too, and take a course in French—she had often said she wished she knew more French. But that would probably mean that Brad would be coming, too. Maybe that wasn't such a great idea. Maybe her mom and Brad would be happier in Africa. Or in Toronto.

"Andrée, promettras-tu de m'écrire s'il te plaît?" asked Cécile, looking a little sad.

"Oui, Cécile. Je te le promets," Andrea replied as she reached for another chunk of the French bread she loved. She would be happy to write to Cécile. She would miss her. Among the many things she would remember about this place was her trip to the bakery every morning. It had been her first job of the day to walk down to the centre of the town before breakfast as the community was coming to life. The bakery always smelled so delicious. She was going to miss a lot of things.

"Et toi, Philippe," Andrea teased, *"tu m'écriras, n'est-ce pas?"*

Philippe looked up at her and laughed in embarrassment. *"Mon anglais . . . pas bon,"* he apologized.

"Ecris en français," Andrea shrugged.

Philippe continued to look embarrassed and returned his gaze to the magazine. He had never, in his entire life, written to a girl.

When it was time to leave for the airport, Philippe offered to carry Andrea's duffle bag out to the Renault. Andrea was wearing her new purple sweatshirt with a map of St. Pierre and Miquelon on it. She felt sure it would be a big hit with the kids at Rattling River High School where she would be a new student a few days from now.

Andrea was surprised that Philippe had decided to go to the airport with them. As the car pulled away from the curb, she looked back nostalgically at Auberge Cécile and silently said good-bye to the orange cat sitting on the fence.

Cécile steered a careful slalom course through the

narrow streets of St. Pierre. As they passed the familiar houses and shops, Andrea glanced at them wistfully. They drove past the Gendarmerie National—the place where this adventure had begun so dismally only a couple of months earlier. She remembered how angry Uncle Cyril had been at being arrested by mistake, and how scared she and Jeff had been. Yet everything had turned out so well. She recalled something her uncle had often said: "Bad beginnings, good endings." She had never quite believed it until now but—was this the end of something or only the beginning?

All too soon the flight to St. John's was being called. Andrea hugged Cécile, who kept on chatting about the trip she and Philippe were planning to visit Philippe's brother and his family in Newfoundland at Christmas time. Cécile was determined to visit her new-found cousins, too—Pearl and Cyril, Jeff and Matthew . . . and Andrea, and lots of other yet unknown relatives in Anderson's Arm.

Philippe also gave Andrea a hug. And then, to her utter amazement, he kissed her goodbye, once on each cheek in the French way. "I *will* write to you," he said shyly. "I will write to you . . . in English."

"Et moi, je t'écrirai en français."

"Promise?" he winked.

"Je te le promets," she smiled.

She turned and walked out to the departure gate and then to the waiting plane.

Soon the French Isles would be behind her . . . but never to be forgotten.

ACKNOWLEDGEMENTS

My thanks to Mary Elliott for her invaluable assistance; to Valerie Smith for her careful scrutiny of the passages in French; to Jean-Pierre Andrieux, who shared with me his boundless knowledge of St. Pierre et Miquelon; to Robin Long, who provided me with a place to work; and to Farley, who—as always—encouraged me.